Spirits and Liqueurs

FABER BOOKS ON WINE

General Editor: Julian Jeffs

Bordeaux by David Peppercorn
Burgundy by Anthony Hanson
Italian Wines by Philip Dallas
Port by George Robertson
Sherry by Julian Jeffs
Vineyards in England and Wales by George Ordish
Wines of Germany by Frank Schoonmaker
(rev. Peter Sichel)
Wines of Portugal by Jan Read
Wines of the Rhône by John Livingstone-Learmonth
and Melvyn C. H. Master
Wines of Spain by Jan Read

SPIRITS AND LIQUEURS

PETER A. HALLGARTEN

faber and faber

First published in 1979
by Faber and Faber Limited
3 Queen Square London WC1N 3AU
This new and revised edition
first published in Faber Paperbacks 1983
Printed in Great Britain by
Redwood Burn Ltd Trowbridge Wiltshire
All rights reserved

British Library Cataloguing in Publication Data

Hallgarten, Peter A.
Spirits and liqueurs.—2nd ed.
1. Liqueurs
I. Title
641.2'5 TP611

ISBN 0-571-13057-7

To Elaine

Contents

9

Contents

Figures

Foreword to First Edition

My unpremeditated and totally unexpected involvement in liqueur manufacture began in 1961 with the sudden resignation of the Company Compounder. As a recently qualified chemist, I was selected to take over current manufacture and complete partial productions. Once involved, the fascination and wonder of liqueurs gripped my full interest and I have been researching old products and developing new liqueurs since that time.

Starting with the return of Glen Mist to Scotland in 1963, I launched 'Royal Mint-Chocolate Liqueur' at Hotelympia in 1966. Its instant success encouraged me to develop a 'Royal Family' of liqueurs, of which there are now nine completely new and unique flavours, exported to many countries from France, where they are distilled and produced to my original formulae.

My thanks are especially due to Julian Jeffs for his patience with my delayed production of this manuscript, to my wife Elaine for writing Chapter 29, to Aleck Crighton, Mal Harris and Sir Guy Fison for reading the chapters on Irish whiskey, American whiskey and rum, to the Scotch Whisky Association and Food from France for statistical information, to my friends in the trade for assisting with background information of their agency products, and, finally, to my hard-working secretaries who interpreted my tapes and handwriting in producing this manuscript.

London, 1978   P.H.

Foreword to Second Edition

Since 1978 there have been significant changes in the market for spirits and liqueurs. The popularity of white spirits continues to grow, and liqueurs have received a new stimulus from the large-scale introduction and successful promotion of dairy liqueurs. The only dark cloud overhead (and hovering continually on the horizon) is higher excise taxation, which not only increases prices but also restricts consumer choice.

Nevertheless, the popularity of liqueurs persists. Many new products have been launched since 1978, a large number of which have been well received and are included in this new edition of *Spirits and Liqueurs*. Liqueurists continue to produce exciting new flavours, to titillate consumers' palates and to challenge bartenders to concoct novel and even more exotic cocktails and mixed drinks. Long may this trend continue.

London, 1983   P.H.

PART I

I
History of Distillation and Liqueur Production

Hippocrates is said to have practised the art of distillation and the blending of herbs and aromatic plants in the fifth century B.C., but the product may have been a crude vermouth based on wine and not on spirit. Such early concoctions based on aromatized wine were allegedly very potent and inebriating, and therefore fit only for the strongest of men! Five hundred years later Pliny, the famous Roman naturalist, reported distillation and spoke of a Faustino wine, which burned 'De Faustino vino flamma accendi'—and there is no doubt that the ancients skilfully extracted liquid perfume from aromatic plants. Bas-reliefs representing alembics (distillation vessels) were even found in the Temple of Memphis.

It is of course true that liqueurs have both digestive and curative properties, and the herbal wines of the Middle Ages were produced by steeping herbs in grape juice; absinthe, aloes, aniseed, hyssop, myrtle, centaury, rosemary, sage and many more were used. Enthusiastic descriptions are frequently found in the literature of the time, and these herbal wines were indispensable to doctors as prescriptions for the sick; the best were known as *vins herbes* and contained honey and Asian spices. But such publications were available only to the small group able to read and write. Anyone engaging in such arts in mediaeval times acquired a very doubtful reputation for devilry, and many a publication was burnt together with its author.

Liqueurs as we know them, however, are thought to have been invented by monks who, frequently acting as medical men, were interested in herbs and plants, and through appreciating the products of Mother Nature discovered the beauty and benefits of liqueurs.

Dioscorides, a celebrated Greek doctor of the first century A.D., indicated the first primitive distillation apparatus; there is no doubt that the Arabs also had a knowledge of these processes. It was not until around A.D. 800, however, when human ingenuity evolved the process of distillation, that a livelier choice of alcoholic beverages became possible. An Arabian alchemist named Jabir Ibn Hayyan, known to the West as Geber, is generally credited with this feat, and it may have been he who suggested the name for its most effective result. 'Alcohol' is, at any rate, a word of Arabic derivation and stems from 'alkuhl'. The latter originally referred to the eye cosmetic made of powdered antimony, but with time and use it too came to mean any fine-ground substance, then 'essence' and, ultimately, the essential spirit of wine. A dissenting opinion advanced by nineteenth-century temperance leaders held that the proper root of the word 'alcohol' was the Arabic *alghul* meaning ghost or evil spirit.

How Geber was led to accomplish the isolation of alcohol is uncertain. His writings on distillation, which reached mediaeval Europe under the title *Liber Investigationes Magisteri*, gave only a rambling account of his aim and general technique. Indeed, his style was so elaborate and ponderous that it persuaded Samuel Johnson to record in his *Dictionary of the English Language* that the etymological seed of 'gibberish' was 'Geber'.

The Arabs learned the art of distilling from the Egyptians, who distilled wine. Distillation of many kinds of fermented liquids, such as grape-date wine, fruit wine, etc., was known. The Arabs also learned from the Egyptians how to produce rose water from rose petals macerated in alcohol. This was an article of merchandise among the Persians in the ninth century A.D. Rose water was not only a popular raw material for use in cosmetics, but was also employed as a condiment for sweets which are still enjoyed in the Middle East.

Avicennes, an Arab philosopher-doctor born in A.D. 980, discussed two alcoholic products in his writings, and Rhazes, a famous Persian physician somewhat earlier is said to have described, exactly, three distillations. The Chinese are recorded as producing 'alaki' (araki) from rice wines in the thirteenth century, but are thought to have done so as early as 800 B.C.

18

The Chinese, in fact, had discovered the art of distilling spirits some two thousand years before our era. According to Legge's Chinese Classics there is in the Shoo-King, or history, the text of an Imperial Edict addressed to 'Ye people of the Land of Mei', which is believed to have been promulgated about 1116 B.C., and the title of which is *The Announcement about Drunkenness*. A commentator on this Edict, one Soo-Ting-po, says: 'Spirits are what men will not do without. To prohibit them and secure a total abstinence from them is beyond the power even of sages. Here, therefore, we have warnings about them.' If the compilers of dates are to be trusted, it was fully three thousand years ago that the Chinese sages first declared that temperance was a virtue, that all men were not virtuous, and that no man could be virtuous who was not free.

As time went by the products were improved, and with each generation, as the secrets were handed down, slight variations were bound to occur. Communication was by word of mouth and formulae were hardly ever written down. Nowadays, of course, formulae can have great commercial value, and with the risks of modern life, most holders of liqueur secrets make use of bank vaults to ensure continuity of their famous products.

French researchers believe that Arnauld de Villeneuve in the thirteenth century rediscovered *eaux-de-vie* distillation. He wrote that the distillate should be kept in golden vessels, so as not to impair its quality, and recorded that *eaux-de-vie* in which rosemary and sage had been steeped were soothing to the nerves! Arnauld's conception of alcohol was practical in the extreme. To his dazzled eyes it was the solution to the problem that was then the chief concern of European science; it was the philosopher's stone, the universal panacea, the key to life everlasting: 'Limpid and well flavoured red and white wine', were comments incorrectly attributed to him, 'is to be digested twenty days in a closed vessel, by heat, and then to be distilled in a sand bath with a very gentle fire. The true water of life will come over in precious drops, which, being rectified by three or four successive distillations, will afford the wonderful quintessence of wine. We call it aqua vitae, and this name is remarkably suitable, since it is really a water of immortality. It prolongs life, clears away ill-humours, revives the heart, and maintains youth.'

With Luell he supposedly produced the first recorded French liqueur, *l'eau clairette*, a sweetened *eau-de-vie*, scented with lemon, rose leaves and other aromatic herbs. The product was decorated with specks of gold in the belief that 'nature had endowed gold with the most admirable virtues'. Both Arnauld and Luell lived to be well over seventy, a considerable age for those times, and it is possible that their example was taken as convincing confirmation of the emanation's worth. It is certain that it was rapidly elevated to a place of sovereign prominence in the Christian medicine chest.

German literature seems quite clear that commercial distillation was invented between 1050 and 1150. The work of Magister Salernus, who made 'aqua ardens', is quoted in the twelfth century.

By the fourteenth century much progress had been made in the art of distilling wine, and aqua-vitae (brandy) was beginning to be tolerably well known to the people of France and Germany; no record has come to light so far to show that any spirit was distilled in England at so early a date.

In 1358 Ortholaus gives in his *Pratica Alchimica*, detailed directions for the distillation of wine and for rectifying the first alcohol to result from such distillation. From the publication, at Augsburg, in 1483, of Michael Schreik's treatise *Verzeichniss der augsgebranden Wasser*, it is evident that the use of brandy was no longer confined to medicinal purposes, in Germany, at the time. There is confirmation of this in a decree issued by the municipality of Nuremberg in 1496, forbidding the sale of 'distilled waters' on Sundays and other holidays, in private houses as well as by druggists and other merchants in their shops, or in the market place, in the streets or elsewhere, so as to put a stop to their abuse and excessive consumption.

In the fifteenth century Michel Savonarole is credited with distillation from a metal container and subsequent cooling of the hot vapours in a cold-water bath. In his book *De Aqua Vitae*, he described the work of the Franciscan monk de Rupescissa with wine, roots, fruits and herbs.

'Aqua Vitae is commonly called the mistress of all medicines,' wrote Hieronymus Brunschwig, the titan of fifteenth-century German medicine, surgery, and pharmacology. 'It eases the diseases coming from cold. It comforts the heart. It heals all old and new sores on the head. It causes a good colour in a person. It heals baldness and causes the hair to grow well and kills lice and fleas. It cures lethargy. Cotton wet in the same and a little wrung out again and so put in the ears at night going to bed, and a little drunk thereof, is a good against all deafness. It eases the pain in the teeth, and causes sweet breath. It heals the canker in the mouth, in the teeth, in the lips, and in the tongue. It causes the heavy tongue to become light and well-speaking. It heals the short breath. It causes good digestion and appetite for food, and takes away all belching. It draws the wind out of the body. It eases the yellow jaundice, the dropsy, the gout, the pain in the breasts when they be swollen, and heals all diseases in the bladder, and breaks the stone. It withdraws venom that has been taken in meat or in drink, when a little treacle is put thereto. It heals all shrunken sinews, and causes them to become soft and right. It heals the fevers terian and quartan. It heals the bite of a mad dog, and all stinking wounds, when they be washed therewith. It gives also young courage in a person, and causes him to have a good memory. It purifies the five wits of Melancholy and of all uncleanliness.'

Brunschwig's proclamation included, however, a cautionary note. 'It is to be drunk by reason and measure,' he warned. 'That is to understand, five or six drops in the morning, fasting, with a spoonful of wine.'

In mediaeval times the apothecaries sold spices, herbs, seeds and grain, wax articles, and usually home-made sweets as well; not until the fourteenth century did the manufacture of medicaments become the most important part of their business. The first aromatic waters and essential oils were obtained by the apothecaries through steam distillation. By this time distilling apparatus had been developed so far that a start was made on rectification of alcohol and the preparation of alcohol in its pure state. The alchemist Bernhard of Treviso (1400–90) prepared alcohol of nearly 98 per cent by volume; in the end he distilled his alcohol over quicklime. Thaddeus Alderotti (1223–1303) describes the fractional distillation of wine. Similar information is also found in the writings of other alchemists, such as Otholamus Savonarola (the grandfather of the unsuccessful reformer), Brunschwig and others.

By the Middle Ages Italy had also become a liqueur producer, with centres of production in Florence, Venice and Turin. Catherine de Medici is supposed to have enjoyed them and to have made them popular in France, and a liqueur recipe of that time consisting of brandy, water, sugar musk, amber, aniseed and cinnamon is reported to have rejuvenated the ageing Louis XIV. These liqueurs include 'le rossoli', which were liqueurs of many recipes, and 'le populo', which was sweetened wine spirit flavoured with natural products. Lievin Lemnius, a Dutchman, bestows great praises on aqua-vitae in his *Secrets of Nature*, written in the early part of the sixteenth century, thus: 'No liquor, that is ministered unto any use to man's body, is either lighter or more piercing, or more preserveth and defendeth all things from corruption . . .' The use of spirits must have been quite common on the Continent, since the same author goes on to say: 'The use of Aqua Vitae has grown so common in Nether Germany and Flanders, that, more freely than is profitable to health, they take and drink of it.' Elsewhere in northern Europe it was taken, if anything, even more freely.

In 1559, when Peter Morwyng published his *Treasure of Evonymous*, wine was no longer distilled solely by apothecaries and for medicinal purposes; there were already a certain number of 'distillers', in London, who distilled spirits of a kind from the unsound wines and wine-lees which vintners and coopers were only too pleased to sell to them at very low rates. Morwyng claimed that spirit distilled from either good or bad wine was equally good, since whatever was bad in unsound wine could not be its spirit, its soul, but merely its grosser body: 'Burning water, or aqua vitae, is drawn oute of wyne, but wyth us out of the wyne lies [lees] onely, specially of them that sell it, and by this onely almost get their livying. And peradventure it is never a whit the worse that it is drawne oute of lees; for Lullus teacheth that it may be well distilled of corrupt wine; yea, if it be distilled often it shal be made the more effectuall (that is to say) hotter and drier.'

He also gives us an idea of what to expect from aqua-vitae: 'It helpeth red and duskish eyes. It is good for them that have the falling sickness if they drink it. It cureth the palsy if they be onoynted therewith. It sharpenth the wit, it restoreth memori. It maketh men merry and preserveth youth. It putteth away francins, ring worms and all spots of the face, etc. It is merveylous

22

profitable for frantic men and such as be melancholy. It expelleth poison. The smell therefore burnt, killeth flies and cold creeping beasts. It restoreth wine, that is turned or putrefied.

'It is most wholesome for the stomake, the harte and the liver; it nourisheth blood; it agreeth merveylously and most with man's nature. . . . Yea, it changeth the affection of the mind; it taketh away sadness, pensiveness; it maketh men merri, witty, and encreaseth audacitie. . . . To conclude, it bringeth a good smell and taste also to any wine, be it never so evil or corrupt, and good wine also it maketh it better.'

Even the much maligned absinthe, or something very similar to it, was known in England at the end of the sixteenth century, being made, so Peter Morwyng tells us, with dried leaves of wormwood steeped in equal parts of Malmsey wine and 'burning water thrice distilled'.

In 1576 another book on distillation, *The Newe Jewell of Health*, was sold out as soon as published. This was Conrad Gesner's book on distillation translated by a George Baker, who published it himself. By then the demand for aqua-vitae had grown so much that 'even good wine' had to be distilled to meet the demand: 'The burning water, or water of life, is sometimes distilled out of pleasant and good wine, as the whyte or the red, but oftener drawn out of the wine lees, of a certain eager savour, or corrupt wyne. . . . Further, when out of pure wyne a water of life is distilled, I hear, says Conrad Gesner, that out of a great quantity of good wine, a little yeld or quantity of burning water is to be distilled; but out of the lees of wine, a much [greater] yeld and quantity [is] gathered; an out of wine Alsatico, is not so commendable as aqua vitae distilled.'

As the demand for spirits grew, methods of distillation improved together with the distillers' profits, and the more enterprising of them also experimented with a number of cordials or blends of wine, spirit and various flavourings, from herbs, spices, or such fruits and plants as were then available. In *The Newe Jewell of Health* these concoctions are called 'laudable confortable, commendable and singular cordial wynes', and their use is recommended in a variety of surprising emergencies. Thus, if a man be 'wholly mad', cordial wines might bring him back to reason; they also dispelled evil thoughts and prevented all 'evyl congitations coming to minde'; more wonderful still, they are said to have restored sight to the blind, and it is claimed that they 'strengtheneth any weake member of man's body'. Many of these cordial wines of course were sweetened.

The first brandy 'aqua-vitae' reached England by way of troops returning from an expedition to the Low Countries in 1585.

'In their endeavours to meet the increasing demand for cheaper spirits, English distillers now began to use, in lieu of wine and wine lees, hog's wash and such starting materials for making aqua vitae, and they continued to do so until 1593, the year of the plague. In former ages, it had been usual to attribute a visitation of the plague to the Jews, who were said to have poisoned the wells, or indeed, to any source other than that filth of the people and their dwellings that fostered it. On this occasion the distillers were accused of having, in effect, poisoned the *aqua vitae* that was frequently used as an antidote. Accordingly they were "rectified", as it was termed, under a patent, granted to Drake, for the monopoly of the sale of spirits but this patent was subsequently abolished, with the other monopolies, by the Queen, in 1601, and Cecil, in announcing the abolition to the House of Commons in a humorous speech, congratulated those who had cold stomachs on the liberty they had acquired in free indulgence in *aqua vitae, aqua composita*, and other waters.'*

In 1638, in the reign of King Charles I, the Worshipful Company of Distillers was incorporated in London, the charter of which conferred upon the Company extensive powers and important duties in the regulation of the Trade of Distillers and Vinegar-makers, and of those engaged in the preparation of artificial and strong waters in the Cities of London and Westminster. In 1747 French distillers came within the jurisdiction of the local courts for the control of the preparation of drugs and herbal remedies. After the Revolution the French distillers established themselves with rules for apprenticeships, admission as a *chef d'oeuvre* and dispensation for sons of 'masters'. Widows were permitted to work but not to be apprenticed.

Throughout the eighteenth century, following the policy introduced by William of Orange, everything that could be done to

* *A History of Taxation and other Taxes in England from the earliest times to the year 1885.* Stephen Dowell, London 1888.

kill the taste of the people of England for the wines of France and all that was French *was* done. There were, of course, many apostles of the grape, who warned their contemporaries of the dangers of alcoholism, but their warnings were not heeded. The anonymous author of *A Friendly Admonition to the Drinkers of Brandy and other Distilled Spirituous Liquors*, published in London in 1733, described all spirits as the masterpiece of the devil, and declared that: 'Physicians observe that these distilled spirituous liquors, which are inflamed by repeated distillation, are, in a manner, direct poison to human bodies.' In the same period Dr Shaw, a stalwart champion of the grape, declared that wine 'makes a Lamb of a Lion and changes a Vulture to a Dove, purifying and transforming souls into a temper wholly divine'. The title of his book, published in London in 1724, is as good as a preface: *The Juice of the Grape is Wine.*

The monks of Italian monasteries changed from being medicinal distillers to producers of fragrant waters, the first of which as already mentioned, was supplied by rose water. The fragrant peel of Aurantiaceae fruit, such as lemons, bergamots and oranges, as well precious orange flowers, were added thereto. Orange-flower oil became a fashionable perfume (under the name of Neroli Essence) around 1680 because it was favoured by the Duchess of Flavio Orsini, Princess of Neroli, near Rome.

Seventeenth-century literature has frequent references to ratafias and similar products being served, and there are several German treatises on the manufacture of wines and their distillation. Recorded liqueurs from the eighteenth century include aquavit flavoured with angelica, cardamom, citrus fruits, coffee and various herbal flavours. Persiko was a peach-leaf distillate, and aniseed, rose and celery ratafias were produced. The finished liqueurs were coloured with natural products and even filtered before sale.

The nineteenth century saw great progress made in distillation and the acceptance of new techniques. Areas became famous for special products: Amsterdam (curaçao), Bordeaux (anisette), Marseilles (absinthe), Grenoble (ratafias), Dijon (cassis), Paris (all liqueurs) and, of course, many monasteries all over France produced their own specialities. Some of these liqueurs used more than a hundred different ingredients to produce the final product.

It is interesting that the magnificent French green and yellow herb liqueurs, which originated in monasteries, have not been equalled by any other liqueur-producing country—most of which are Protestant!

The first French liqueur was probably *l'eau clairette*, of Villeneuve, already described, and then came the liqueurs of Montpelier, of Lorraine (*parfait amour*) and, of course, the ratafias, cherry and blackcurrant, which still retain their popularity. Local distilleries were started in mountain regions, where the compounding and distillation were facilitated by the ready availability of spices and fruits.

Although France and Holland are the best known, all fruit-growing countries produce their own liqueurs and frequently *eaux-de-vie* as well. In many cases the latter are 'whiskies' from cereals. Emphasis in this book has obviously been placed on liqueurs that are well known, mainly in the United Kingdom and the U.S.A., many of which have become 'brand leaders' to the exclusion of similar products, which, through commercial considerations, have not received the support of advertising.

Nevertheless, there are many very fine liqueurs produced in Germany, Italy, the East European countries, Spain, Australia, Japan, and other countries which are not exported because they would not be commercially viable propositions in competition with equivalent products that have been known for decades. A few Israeli liqueurs, which are manufactured in accordance with dietary laws of food preparation and are thus kosher, are exported and can therefore be enjoyed by religious Jews elsewhere. I can recall the superb Australian liqueurs that were imported just after the war, which were thoroughly enjoyed until the Dutch and French liqueurs returned, when the old European names rapidly replaced the new ones. The British liqueur industry is thriving, although on a more rational basis than before the war. Many products are no longer being manufactured, but the best play an important role in the export drive.

One of the most interesting developments of the past decade is the manufacture, under licence, of Dutch and French liqueurs in the U.S.A. and recently of Dutch liqueurs in Australia, using local spirit but the original flavour concentrate, which is shipped in bulk. Some famous gins are rectified in New Jersey, and in certain countries Scotch malt whisky is blended with local grain spirit, producing a 'Scotch-type whiskey' which can be very palatable—the line, however, must be drawn when these whiskies are represented as pure Scotch whisky. The Scotch Whisky Association is most vigilant and takes action against fraudulent representation as true Scotch whisky.

The secret of a good liqueur is its flavour, its perfume, the fine balance of the alcohol (which must be present but not obvious) and the cohesive sweetness—essentially a smooth homogeneous liquid, of enticing and entrancing perfume and colour. The word liqueur is derived from the Latin *liquefacere*, to melt, make liquid or dissolve, and is a solution in which the essential elements must be intricately and irreversibly mixed and dissolved.

Thousands of liqueurs are known, produced in many countries in most parts of the world, and it would be impossible to name them all in this book. Those that are known to me are discussed in a later section. Turning back the pages of history it is amusing to note some of the many liqueurs invented to celebrate a special occasion or designed to appear as elixirs of medicines or solely to titillate the imagination: *Venus Oil, Cream of the Virgin, Harems' Delight, The Good Minded Empress, Parfait Amour*, and many others.

The Bols museum, which has been perfectly transplanted from the centre of Amsterdam to their new site at Nieuw Vennep, has several dozen of these delightful concoctions on show. *Illicit Love* is self-explanatory. *Hansje in de Kelder* (Johnny in the cellar) was the celebration drink when a young couple announced a future happy event to their parents. The traditional hexagonal silver salver (one side for each participant) incorporates in the centre the figure of a baby which rises up as the dish is filled with the liqueur. After the ceremony, the cup was placed in the window for neighbours to see the good news.

2

Scotch Whisky

～～～∂∽～～～

The history of malt whisky is the story of an ancient cult practised throughout the glens of Scotland. The output of the stills in the small crofts was originally for home enjoyment and for the resuscitation of weary travellers. There are few manufacturing processes in the world that can produce such a magnificent product from the simplest ingredients and the most fundamental techniques. Yet this is achieved among the hills and valleys of the Scottish Highlands, for it is here, amid the peat and the fresh spring waters from the hills, that the Scots discovered the secret of making *uisge beath*—the water of life.

It will never be known when and how distilling began in Scotland, but it is now considered virtually certain that the art was brought to Scotland by missionary monks from Ireland. The Irish are well recorded as manufacturing spirit when they were invaded by the English at the end of the twelfth century. The siting of distilleries on the west coast of Scotland where early monastic communities existed reinforces this theory. No doubt the popularity of whisky spread with its use as a medicine 'for the preservation of health, prolongation of life and for the relief of colic, dropsy, palsy, smallpox as well as many other ailments'.

The actual name 'whisky' gradually emerged from the Gaelic, and the earliest recorded reference to distilling is in the Exchequer Rolls for 1494: 'Eight bolls of malt to Friar Cor wherewith to make Aquavitae.' In the early 1500s whisky was available at the court of James IV.

Control of production became essential because impure materials could have caused serious illness, and in 1505 the Edinburgh College of Surgeons were asked to supervise distillation in their City, it being decreed that only barbers and surgeons were allowed to dispense it. An individual whisky, Ferintosh, was

28

mentioned by John Knox: 'the sociable practice of Highlandmen in all ages, to seal satisfy and wash down every compact or bargain in good old Ferintosh': and again in 1690, when an 'ancient brewery of aquavitie in Cromaby' was destroyed by the Jacobites. Forbes, the owner, was compensated with permission to distil free of duty, a privilege cancelled in 1784.

Government has apparently always interfered with production; as early as 1597, with fears of famine after a poor barley crop, distillation was restricted to 'Lords of Barony and Gentlemen of such degree'. Even in 1664 distillers suffered taxation when the Scots Parliament carried a duty of 2s 8d per Scots pint on aquavitae, or other strong liquor. The introduction of taxation was inevitably coupled with tax avoidance and often violent obstruction of the Revenue Officers. It was not, however, until 1784 that a licence act made distilling illegal—a most unpopular arrangement which was ignored by many Highlanders. Eventually, licence fees were paid and excise duty levied—resented as much by today's distillers as by those in the early nineteenth century. It was the Duke of Gordon, himself a large landowner, who in 1823 argued in the Lords that it was impossible to stop Highlanders distilling. However, if realistic and reasonable facilities were provided for the legal manufacture of whisky, he and his fellow landowners would do their best to suppress distillation and also encourage their tenants to have licences for their stills. In the same year an act was passed which allowed distillation on payment of duty of 2s on every gallon distilled, and also required a licence fee of £10 for all stills larger than 40-gallon capacity. The size of the illicit production problem is measured by three thousand detections in 1824 in the Elgin area alone!

By the mid nineteenth century Scotland's malt whiskies were marketed south of the border as well as all over Scotland. Customs and Excise in 1853 permitted vatting of different years' whiskies from the same distillery on a duty-paid basis and, in 1860, vatting in bond of whiskies from different distilleries, steps to ensure a consistently high quality.

Conflict and problems in the Scotch industry abound. It was not only the teetotallers who provoked quarrels; there was also a war of words between the malt and the grain whisky distillers. In the early 1860s Andrew Usher started the use of grain whisky in the production of blends that were lighter and smoother than the highly flavoured pure malts, and it was the popularity of these blends which deeply disturbed the traditional malt whisky distillers.

The malt distillers, just over a century ago, formed their own North of Scotland Malt Distillers Association to discuss and combat the problems of their day—water pollution and over-production, which are not unknown as discussion points even today; and the 'adulteration of their original whisky with tasteless grain—the new silent spirit'. As the industry grew in size and fame it became essential to protect the name of Scotch throughout the world, and the Whisky Association (now the Scotch Whisky Association) was formed in 1917.

In 1875 the malt distillers produced an anti-adulteration of malt (by grain whisky) campaign with the theme 'the nature, substance and quality of the article demanded', which became part of the 1875 Sale of Food and Drugs Act. The adulteration argument was finally settled in 1909, but in the interim period attempts to ban the blending of malt and grain whisky failed until a successful action was brought by Islington Borough in London against several publicans and off-licencees. The Court produced a verdict in essence naming blends as counterfeit. At that stage, however, a well-matured grain from the Cambus Distillery was launched, and its marketing brought the main problem to a crisis point which resulted in the setting up of a Royal Commission in 1908. The Commission produced their now famous verdict in 1909 after long meetings at which the Commissioners heard evidence from distillers, scientists and lawyers. 'Our general conclusion, therefore, on this part of the inquiry is that "Whisky" is a spirit obtained by distillation from a mash of cereal grains, saccharified by the diastase of malt; that Scotch Whisky is Whisky as above defined, distilled in Scotland, and that Irish Whiskey is Whiskey as above defined, distilled in Ireland.'

Grain whisky distillation (see p. 33) was now an accepted method of Scotch production—the summary differentiated neither between types of still permitted (pot or patent) nor between the cereal types (barley for malt whisky; barley and maize for grain whisky). The problems for Scotch whisky continued, however: in 1917 the Finance Bill presented by Lloyd George (who in 1915 had said 'drink is doing more damage in this war than all the German submarines put together') introduced a three-year maturation period in cask for Scotch whisky. In the 1933 Finance Act, a clause combined the necessity for a three-year maturation period with the summary from the 1909 Royal Commission, but it was not until 1952 that the Customs and Excise Act gave statutory definition for Scotch whisky: 'Spirits described as Scotch Whisky shall not deem to correspond to that description unless they have been obtained in Scotland from a mash of cereal grain saccharified by the diastase of malt and have been matured in warehouse in cask for a period of at least three years.'

In the early 1940s American distillers attempted to discredit grain whisky by claiming it was neutral spirit. After much litigation it was agreed that 'Scotch Grain Whiskies are lighter bodied Whiskies, distilled from maize and matured similarly to malt whiskies.'

The legal definition of Scotch Whisky

Scotch whisky has been defined in law since 1909. The definition is to be found in the Finance Act 1969, Schedule 7, paragraph 1. This was amended in 1979 and 1980 to take account of the introduction of the system of alcoholic strength measurement recommended by the international Organization of Legal Metrology and the requirement that maturation must take place in Scotland. Current British legislation states that:

(a) the expression 'whisky' or 'whiskey' shall mean spirits which have been distilled from a mash of cereals which have been—
  (i) saccharified by the diastase of malt contained therein with or without other natural diastases approved for the purpose by the Commissioners; and
  (ii) fermented by the action of yeast; and
  (iii) distilled at an alcoholic strength (computed in accordance with section 2 of the Alcoholic Liquor Duties Act 1979) less than 94·8 per cent in such a way that the distillate has an aroma and flavour derived from the materials used, and which have been matured in wooden casks in warehouse for a period of at least three years;
(b) the expression 'Scotch Whisky' shall mean whisky which has been distilled and matured in Scotland and the expression

'Irish Whiskey' shall mean whiskey which has been distilled and matured in the Republic of Ireland or in Northern Ireland or partly in one and partly in the other;

(c) the expression 'blended whisky', 'blended whiskey', 'blended Scotch Whisky' or 'blended Irish Whiskey' shall mean a blend of a number of distillates each of which separately is entitled to the description whisky, whiskey, Scotch Whisky or Irish Whiskey, as the case may be;

(d) the period for which any blended whisky, blended whiskey, blended Scotch Whisky or blended Irish Whiskey shall be treated as having been matured shall be taken to be that applicable in the case of the most recently distilled of the spirits contained in the blend.

The inclusion of the maximum strength of distillation in the definition was essential to combat American interests which stated that grain whisky was used at the same high strength (95 per cent alcohol) as is normal in the production of neutral spirit.

There are very many wine merchants who stock a large range of individual malt whiskies, and most well-frequented public houses and hotel bars have an excellent selection for their patrons. For travellers in Scotland there is a full range of labelled bottles (empty) which can be examined in the Whisky Room at Cameron House on the shores of Loch Lomond, near the Deer Park. Apart from the whiskies, the house is most worthy of a visit for its collection of paintings, furniture and *objets d'art*.

The most difficult problem for distillers and blenders (brand owners) is to forecast future market trends and to judge their own requirements for four to six years ahead. Production of Scotch whisky has always exceeded consumption requirements and allows for an increased demand in the future and also for the very large evaporation losses during maturation in warehouse. In their planning, producers give very careful consideration to the enormous cost of financing stock, not only in terms of production, but also storage and insurance costs and evaporation losses. Stockholding must therefore be a judicious mixture of crystal-ball gazing and reasonable statistical assumptions.

Branch Water

A term for water from a small tributary stream said to be the only suitable dilutant for the finest whiskies.

PRODUCTION

Grain Whisky: Scotch, Irish and American

Representative of the manufacturing process is that followed at the North British Distillery Company, which was founded in 1885 by leading members of the Scotch Whisky trade with the aim of supplying the trade with grain whisky of consistent quality for blending. Two cereals are used—barley and maize. The barley is malted: first it is soaked in water in one of the Distillery's sixteen steeps; then it is left to germinate in 'saladin boxes', through which air of controlled temperature and humidity is circulated. Next, it is carefully dried in kilns. The diastatic property of malted barley will convert the starch in unmalted grain into sugar.

The maize provides the bulk of the starch for the distilling process. It is ground into flour, which is then steam-pressure cooked so that the particles swell and burst. All the starch in the maize is thus fully exposed to the diastase of the malted barley and converted into sugar when these two ingredients are mixed with hot water in the 'mash tun'. The 'worts', as the saccharine water is called, are run off through coolers to the fermenting-vessels, or 'wash-backs'. The residual grain, or 'draff', is removed and sold as cattle food.

There are twenty wash-backs, each of 40,000 gallons' capacity. Yeast from the Distillery's own culture plant is placed in the wash-backs to start fermentation. The yeast splits the sugar content of the worts into alcohol and carbon dioxide. After two days, the 'wash' is transferred to the stills for the recovery of the alcohol.

The patent stills used for grain whiskies are of the continuous Coffey type. The still consists of two large vertical columns placed consecutively, one the analyser, the second the rectifier. Each column consists of a series of perforated plates. The cold wash enters at the top of the analyser and meets steam introduced under pressure from the bottom. This vaporizes the alcohol and other volatile components which, in turn, are condensed by the new cold wash, which itself is warmed in the process of heat exchange in the rectifier. The vapours, or 'feints', are carried to the rectifier column, while the spent wash is run off to dreg ponds,

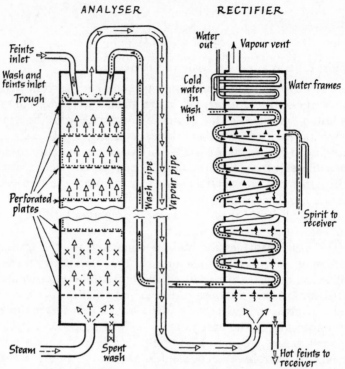

ANALYSER   RECTIFIER

1. Coffey still for grain whisky
North British Distillery Company diagram

where a certain amount of grain sediment from the wash is recovered for the manufacture of cattle cake.

As the feints rise through the frames of the rectifier column they cool and condense. By careful regulation of the temperature the ethyl alcohol in the feints is made to condense at a particular level. The resulting liquid is grain whisky. From here the whisky is run through a spirit pipe, which is immersed in water in the worm tub, to cool further before being collected in the spirits receiver. The spirit in the receiver is of much higher strength than is required for potable grain whisky. It is run off to vats in the spirit store and reduced by water to a strength suitable for maturing—usually 11° over proof. The excisemen check the weight, strength and temperature of the spirit as the casks are filled. The exact content of each cask is gauged in gallons at proof strength. The casks are then stored in warehouse to mature until required. In Scotland, the spirit may be called whisky after three years' maturing.

This type of distillation is continuous and requires much less labour and skill than does pot-still distillation. Although the plant is called the 'Coffey' still, the basic method was in fact invented by Robert Stein, a Scottish distiller, who patented the process in 1826. Four years later Aeneas Coffey, an Irish exciseman in Dublin, greatly improved the method and it is his name that remains linked to the process.

Malt Whisky

Scotch malt whisky is made from barley, much of which is locally grown, although today a great amount is imported. Each distillery makes certain that only best-quality barley goes into the malting stage, and inferior quality is rejected.

Production of malt whisky can be broken down in well-defined separate stages—malting, mashing, fermenting, distilling and finally maturing.

The vital factors in determining quality are the standards of the raw material, the origin of the peat used in the fires that dry the germinated barley, and the pure softness of the water from the Scottish burns. Whatever the quality of the raw materials, however, the final factor in production is the skill of the distiller, who works by instinct and experience. There is no doubt that the production of malt whisky is an art; attempts at scientific reproduction have proved unsuccessful. The processes involved are of course well understood but the mystery of the unique and characteristic flavour of whiskies from different yet closely situated distilleries remains unsolved and no one has been able to produce a spirit with the flavour of true Scotch whisky outside Scotland.

Much of the barley used in present-day whisky distilling is received at the distillery already malted, but some traditional distillers continue to carry out the malting process on their own premises.

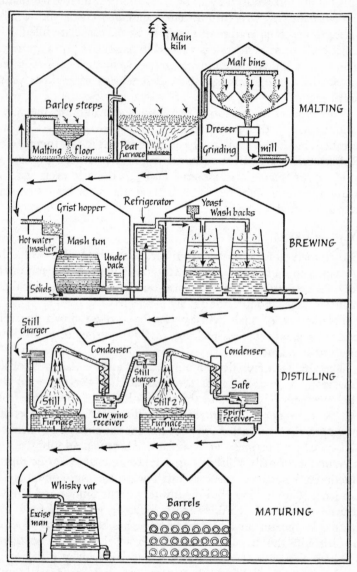

2. Scotch malt whisky distillery, based on Dr McDowall's diagram

MALTING

After elimination of inferior grain, the barley is softened by thorough steeping in water for two or three days. It is then spread over the stone floor of the malting house, where it is kept warm and moist, and germination begins. Germination usually takes seven to ten days, but may take three weeks, and should be a steady process. The roots that form may inter-weave, and in order to prevent this and aerate the grain, the 'floor' is turned at least twice daily, carefully to avoid any damage; the workers use long wooden shovels called 'shiels'. The grain must be kept moist and temperature control is important. During the process soluble starch in the barley is converted into sugars mainly maltose, by enzyme action.

The sprouting grain is now heated in a kiln over a peat fire, which halts germination and dries the grain for milling. The peat smoke gives a characteristic flavour that remains right through the following processes, the unmistakable flavour of Scotch. The flavour of the whisky is much dependent upon the kilning process.

MASHING

The kilned malt is ground into 'grist', thoroughly mixed with warm water. The water used at this stage, as in the original soaking of the barley, is only the purest spring water, often exclusive to one distillery. The residual husks are removed for use as cattle feed. The sweet mixture, known as 'wort', is now fermented by the addition of yeast, after which it contains alcohol and other products, including by-products of the fermentation and the coincidental bacterial action.

The 'wash-backs' (fermenting-vessels) are vats that can hold between 10,000 and 14,000 gallons. Some distillers prefer to use steel-lined vessels for the fermenting process, but the traditional distilleries use pinewood vats. When fermentation begins, the yeast reacts with the sugary content of the liquor to produce a weak alcohol. The violent action of the yeast necessitates rotating wooden arms, known as 'switchers', at the top of each wash-back, to 'cut' the surface froth and prevent overflow from the vats.

The weakly alcoholic solution 'wash' (approximately 10 per cent) is pumped into the wash still, where distillation produces a distillate, also weakly alcoholic—'low wines' (approximately 20 per cent alcohol). 'Low wines' are re-distilled in a different still, and only the middle fraction is useful spirit—Scotch malt whisky at approximately 70 per cent alcohol.

In the glass-fronted spirit safe the stillman can see the resultant spirit running, but he rejects these first runnings as being unsuitable, containing too many impurities and raw essences. Gradually, as distillation continues, the stillman can gauge when the spirit is ready. The stillman makes what is known as the 'middle cut'—the birth of true Scotch whisky—and begins to run that spirit into the receiving vessel. When exactly he makes that 'cut' varies from distillery to distillery. Two whiskies made next door to each other may be 'cut' at different times. Whatever the decision, it is certain that the resulting spirit is unique to that distillery and that process, and cannot be copied anywhere else in the world.

The first part of the distillation 'heads' and the end part of the distillation 'tails' are known as 'feints', and these are added to the next batch of low wines, their useful contents thus being preserved. These fractions usually contain high proportions of acids, fusel oils and aldehyde contaminants.

Distillers can control, within limits, the flavour of the distillate, and it has been said that mild peat flavour is best produced by slow distillation, whereas heavy peat flavour is obtained by rapid distillation over hotter fires. Modern distilleries of course use steam heat which can be automatically controlled and much more finely regulated than can an open fire. The heating of the 'wash' during the first distillation causes changes in minor constituents, which are vital to the flavour and character of the whisky.

The useful spirit fraction must, of course, be reduced in strength for maturing and 63 per cent is accepted by most distillers. It is most important that pure water is used in reducing the strength of the whisky, and the quality of this water also is important in determining the flavour of the final product.

Four main types of Scotch malt whisky are produced according to their district of distillation:

Highland —Considered the finest malts, light in flavour, delicate in body and smokiness. The Glenlivet and Speyside whiskies are considered the best.

Lowland   —Light-bodied, flavoury.
Campbeltowns —Very full bodied smoky malt whiskies.
Islay   —Very full bodied, smoky flavoured, some-
               times very strong. Excellent blending
               whiskies.

Both malt and grain types of whisky distilled in Scotland are legally entitled only to the term 'spirits' until they have been aged in cask for a minimum of three years, at which time they may be called Scotch whisky. Scotch whisky exported to the U.S.A. must be aged four years in cask.

Maturing in wooden casks is a most important stage in the development of any pot-stilled spirit which contains fusel oils, aldehydes and other intensely flavoured products (congeners), which make the newly distilled spirit sharp in flavour. In cask the whisky is in contact with air and wood, and because of this, physical and chemical changes take place: some compounds oxidize, some interact because of the oxygen of the air, some compounds are absorbed by the wood, and certain compounds and colour are drawn from the wood, and some may interact through a catalytic effect of the tannins or other compounds in the wood. The overall result is that the whisky develops fine bouquet and flavour, becomes slightly coloured and mellows. During the ageing process there is an obvious loss in volume and alcoholic strength through evaporation—the damper the climate, the smaller the loss of volume; the hotter the storage temperature, the higher the loss of volume and strength—accompanied by an increased rate of maturation, though not necessarily a better maturation. For the finest whiskies, distillers prefer to use recently emptied sherry casks.

Many single distillery malt whiskies are now commercially available, usually after lengthy maturing in cask. The finest are sold at eight, ten or twelve years old, and are equal to the finest liqueurs. They are dry of course, without sweetening, usually marketed at higher strength (43/46 per cent) than blended whiskies with attractive labelling that gives the age of the youngest distillation.

Whisky drinking in the early nineteenth century was fairly restricted because the unblended malt whiskies were not to everybody's taste. It was not until the latter part of the century, when

3. Map of the whisky distilleries of Scotland

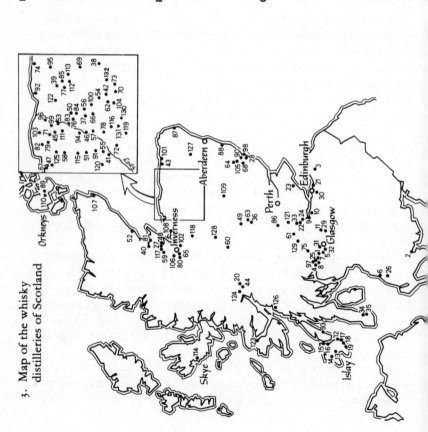

LOWLAND MALT

1. Auchentoshan   *Eadie Cairns Ltd*
2. Bladnoch   *Bladnoch Distillery Ltd*
3. Glenkinchie   *John Haig & Co. Ltd*
4. Inverleven   *Hiram Walker & Sons (Scotland) Ltd*
5. Kinclaith   *Long John Distilleries Ltd*
6. Ladyburn   *Wm Grant & Sons Ltd*
7. Littlemill   *Barton Distilling (Scotland) Ltd*
8. Lomond   *Hiram Walker & Sons (Scotland) Ltd*
9. Rosebank   *The Distillers Agency Ltd*
10. St Magdalene   *John Hopkins & Co. Ltd*
11. Moffat   *Inver House Distillers Ltd*

ISLAY MALT

12. Ardbeg   *Ardbeg Distillery Ltd*
13. Bowmore   *Morrison's Bowmore Distillery Ltd*
14. Bruichladdich   *Bruichladdich Distillery Co. Ltd*
15. Bunnahabhain   *The Highland Distilleries Co. Ltd*
16. Caol Ila   *Bulloch Lade & Co. Ltd*
17. Lagavulin   *White Horse Distilleries Ltd*
18. Laphroaig   *D. Johnston & Co. (Laphroaig) Ltd*
19. Port Ellen   *Low Robertson & Co. Ltd*

GRAIN

20. Ben Nevis   *Ben Nevis Distillery (Fort William) Ltd*
21. Caledonian   *Scottish Grain Distillers Ltd*
22. Cambus   *Scottish Grain Distillers Ltd*
23. Cameronbridge   *Scottish Grain Distillers Ltd*
24. Carsebridge   *Scottish Grain Distillers Ltd*
25. Dumbarton   *Hiram Walker & Sons (Scotland) Ltd*
26. Girvan   *Wm Grant & Sons Ltd*
27. Invergordon   *The Invergordon Distillers Ltd*
28. Lochside   *Macnab Distillers Ltd*
29. Moffat   *Inver House Distillers Ltd*
30. North British   *North British Distillery Co. Ltd*
31. Port Dundas   *Scottish Grain Distillers Ltd*
32. Strathclyde   *Long John Distilleries Ltd*
33. North of Scotland   *North of Scotland Distilling Co. Ltd*

CAMPBELTOWN MALT

34. Glen Scotia A. Gillies & Co. (Distillers) Ltd
35. Springbank J. & A. Mitchell & Co. Ltd

HIGHLAND MALT

36. Aberfeldy John Dewar & Sons Ltd
37. Aberlour-Glenlivet Aberlour-Glenlivet Distillery Co. Ltd
38. Ardmore Wm Teacher & Sons Ltd
39. Aultmore John & Robt Harvey & Co. Ltd
40. Balblair Balblair Distillery Co. Ltd
41. Balmenach John Crabbie & Co. Ltd
42. Balvenie Wm Grant & Sons Ltd
43. Banff Slater, Rodger & Co. Ltd
44. Ben Nevis Ben Nevis Distillery (Fort William Ltd)
45. Ben Riach-Glenlivet The Longmorn-Glenlivet Distilleries Ltd
46. Benrinnes A. & A. Crawford Ltd
47. Benromach J. & W. Hardie Ltd
48. Ben Wyvis The Invergordon Distillers Ltd
49. Blair Athol Arthur Bell & Sons Ltd
50. Caperdonich The Glenlivet & Glen Grant Distillers Ltd
51. Cardow John Walker & Sons Ltd
52. Clynelish Ainslie & Heilbron (Distillers) Ltd
53. Coleburn J. & G. Stewart Ltd
54. Convalmore W. P. Lowrie & Co. Ltd.
55. Cragganmore D. & J. McCallum Ltd
56. Craigellachie White Horse Distillers Ltd
57. Dailuaine Dailuaine-Talisker Distilleries Ltd
58. Dallas Dhu Benmore Distilleries Ltd
59. Dalmore Whyte & Mackay Distillers Ltd
60. Dalwhinnie James Buchanan & Co. Ltd
61. Deanston Deanston Distillers Ltd
62. Dufftown-Glenlivet Arthur Bell & Sons Ltd
63. Edradour Wm Whiteley Ltd
64. Fettercairn Whyte & Mackay Distillers Ltd

65. Glen Albyn Scottish Malt Distillers Ltd
66. Glenallachie Mackinlay-McPherson Ltd
67. Glenburgie-Glenlivet James & George Stodart Ltd
68. Glencadam George Ballantine & Son Ltd
69. Glendronach William Teacher & Son Ltd
70. Glendullan Macdonald Greenlees Ltd
71. Glen Elgin White Horse Distillers Ltd
72. Glenfarclas-Glenlivet J. & G. Grant Ltd
73. Glenfiddich Wm Grant & Sons Ltd
74. Glenglassaugh The Highland Distilleries Co. Ltd
75. Glengoyne Lang Brothers Ltd
76. Glen Grant J. & G. Grant, Glen Grant Ltd
77. Glen Keith-Glenlivet Chivas Bros Ltd
78. Glenlivet, The George & J. G. Smith Ltd
79. Glenlossie John Haig & Co. Ltd
80. Glen Mhor Scottish Malt Distillers Ltd
81. Glenmorangie Macdonald & Muir Ltd
82. Glen Moray-Glenlivet Macdonald & Muir Ltd
83. Glenrothes-Glenlivet The Highland Distilleries Co. Ltd
84. Glen Spey Glen Spey Ltd
85. Glentauchers James Buchanan & Co. Ltd
86. Glenturret Glenturret Distillery Ltd
87. Glenugie Long John Distilleries Ltd
88. Glenury-Royal John Gillon & Co. Ltd
89. Highland Park James Grant & Co. (Highland Park Distillery) Ltd
90. Glenesk Wm Sanderson & Son Ltd
91. Imperial Dailuaine-Talisker Distilleries Ltd
92. Inchgower Arthur Bell & Sons Ltd
93. Isle of Jura Isle of Jura Distillery Co. Ltd
94. Knockando Justerini & Brooks Ltd
95. Knockdhu James Munro & Son Ltd
96. Linkwood John McEwan & Co. Ltd
97. Loch Lomond Barton Distilling (Scotland) Ltd
98. Lochside Macnab Distilleries Ltd
99. Longmorn-Glenlivet The Longmorn-Glenlivet Distilleries Ltd

100. Macallan-Glenlivet Macallan-Glenlivet Ltd
101. Macduff William Lawson Distillers Ltd
102. Millburn Macleay Duff (Distillers) Ltd
103. Miltonduff-Glenlivet George Ballantine & Son Ltd
104. Mortlach George Cowie & Son Ltd
105. North Port Mitchell Brothers Ltd
106. Ord Peter Dawson Ltd
107. Pulteney James & George Stodart Ltd
108. Royal Brackla John Bisset & Co. Ltd
109. Royal Lochnagar John Begg Ltd
110. Scapa Taylor & Ferguson Ltd
111. Speyburn John Robertson & Son Ltd
112. Strathisla Chivas Brothers Ltd
113. Strathmill Justerini & Brooks Ltd
114. Talisker Dailuaine-Talisker Distilleries Ltd
115. Tamdhu-Glenlivet The Highland Distilleries Co. Ltd
116. Tamnavulin-Glenlivet Tamnavulin-Glenlivet Distillery Co. Ltd
117. Teaninich R. H. Thomson & Co. (Distillers) Ltd
118. Tomatin Tomatin Distillers Co. Ltd
119. Tomintoul-Glenlivet Whyte & Mackay Ltd
120. Tormore Long John Distilleries Ltd
121. Tullibardine Tullibardine Distillery Ltd
122. Auchroisk Justerini & Brooks (Scotland) Ltd
123. Tobermory Ledaig Distillery (Tobermory) Ltd
124. Glenlochy Scottish Malt Distillers Ltd
125. Mannochmore John Haig & Co. Ltd
126. Oban John Hopkins & Co. Ltd
127. Glen Garioch The Glen Garioch Distillery Co. Ltd
128. Speyside Speyside Distillery Co. Ltd
129. Glen Foyle Brodie Hepburn Ltd
130. Allt-a'Bhainne Chivas Brothers Ltd
131. Braes of Glenlivet Chivas Brothers Ltd
132. Pittyvaich Arthur Bell & Sons Ltd

grain whisky (which is practically tasteless and characterless) was used to dilute the heavy malt flavour, that whisky became an increasingly popular drink. Different brands are various combinations of malt whiskies and also different ratios of malt to grain whiskies. The skill of the blender produces not only a consistent product but also a quality for each particular country to which his brand is shipped.

3
Irish Whiskey

Irish whiskey was known as *usque baugh* and is supposed to have
been enjoyed by Henry II when he visited Ireland in the twelfth
century. Henry VIII introduced a rough and ready system of
taxation, but by the mid sixteenth century distilling had become
widespread, and it was evident that a more organized form of
control was required. Various methods were attempted, such as a
duty per gallon, a tax on stills and a tax on malt. About two
hundred years ago small stills were outlawed, and the numbers in
production were drastically reduced from over a thousand to less
than a hundred, and from that time the Irish distilling industry
has been characterized by large distilleries, generally much larger
than their counterparts in Scotland.

Irish whiskey became one of the most popular forms of spirit
when the demand for gin was in decline. Principal markets were
in England, the Colonies and of course on its home territory. It
is curious that the Coffey still, patented by the Irishman Aeneas
Coffey, has been adopted much more widely in Scotland than in
Ireland. Some provincial distilleries installed these patent stills,
especially in the northern counties where grain distilleries developed, but the Dublin distilleries on which the reputation of
Irish whiskey is built, were emphatic in their single-minded
support for pot-stills and vehement in their rejection of the patent
still and of the idea of blending the produce from pot and patent.

In 1908 during the hearings of the Royal Commission on
Whisky the Irish Distillers strongly defended their pot-still distillation method, together with several important distillers of malt
whisky from Scotland.

Production was greatly affected by the severe budget of 1909
when excise duty was raised from 9s to 14s 9d per proof gallon;

this tremendous increase resulted in halved consumption and the putting out of business of many of the Irish distillers of the time.

With the formation of the Irish Free State in 1921, the new Irish Government decided to retain the high rate of United Kingdom excise duty of 72s 6d per proof gallon, and the price of whiskey was too high for the rural community. Two other important factors at the time were Prohibition in America and the popularity of Scotch whisky in the English market; the demand for Irish whiskey was severely reduced and the result was more closures, only ten distilleries remaining in production.

In 1966, the three principal remaining family distilling companies, Cork Distilleries, John Jamieson, and John Power, merged to form the present Irish Distillers Group, which more recently has acquired a majority interest in the Old Bushmills Distillery in Northern Ireland, which has one of the oldest distilling licences in the world, dating back to the seventeenth century.

The actual distilling of Irish whiskey is closely related to that of Scotch malt whisky, but there are very important differences in the cereal used as raw material and in the number of distillations and strength of the final product. Normally only indigenous raw materials are used, of which the largest part is barley, only some of which is malted. In the past it was usual to add small quantities of wheat and rye, but at present the addition is a small percentage of oats. The barley which is malted is prepared in traditional manner, but the unmalted barley is subjected to drying and very fine milling, which causes a large amount of barley starch to be exposed by the breaking of the starch cell walls. The addition of a small percentage of oats is apparently due to the fact that when only barley is used there is a loss in yield because of a reduction in the efficiency of the fermentation.

The distillation is in pot-stills, which are larger than the typical Scotch malt still. These stills are traditionally equipped with lyne arms, which have horizontal fraction plate rectifiers, placed before the hot vapours enter the coil for condensation.

Three distillations are used in the manufacture of Irish whiskey, and the distillers work at very high alcoholic strength compared to Scotch malt distillers. The final charge for the second distillation for Scotch malt is in the region of 23/25 per cent, while the charge for the third distillation in Ireland is at about 74 per cent

44

so that the Irish malt whiskey when condensed is at about 86 per cent, compared to Scotch malt whisky at 68/71 per cent.

Pot-still whiskies require a very long time to mature, particularly the Irish whiskeys, and in the past whiskeys of twelve years old were not uncommon. Recently, however, Irish Distillers have reintroduced patent stills for the manufacture of grain whiskeys, and by blending grain whiskeys and malt whiskeys prior to the final pot-still distillation, it has been possible to lighten the character of Irish whiskey without lessening the flavour. Notwithstanding the advent of blended Irish whiskeys, the tradition for malt is still extremely strong in Ireland, where customers looking for whiskey often ask for 'a ball of malt'.

The demand for Irish whiskey is increasing, and a large new distillery has been built at Middleton in County Cork, the first in Ireland for over a century. The new distillery is now functioning well and will eventually produce four to five million gallons annually. The superbly designed plant is built on a site with excellent natural water supply and is a strong visual contrast with the romantic buildings of the old distillery, alas now closed, which houses the world's largest pot-still, with a capacity of 31,000 gallons.

The various types of Irish whiskey are now produced by very careful blending of malt and grain whiskeys prior to the last pot-still distillation and standardization of brands is thus ensured. Middleton in the South and Bushmill in the North are now the only remaining distilleries in Ireland; the latter however produces its blends on the Scottish principle of mixing malt and grain after they have been separately distilled.

Poteen, Pocheen

The name for illicitly distilled Irish whiskey.

4
American Whiskey and Others

Although history recalls that the first distillery in North America was established about 1640 on Staten Island by William Keith, there is no doubt whatsoever that the Pilgrim Fathers introduced beers, wines and liquors when they arrived from Europe. These alcoholic drinks were not only pleasant but beneficial and necessary in the prevention of malaria.

The first settlers in Massachusetts ingeniously prepared fermented drinks from all the fruits that were available; pumpkins, parsnips, grapes, currants and elderberries. They distilled 'strong waters' from plums, cherries, pawpaw, blackberries, wortleberries, persimmons, even potatoes, turnips, carrots and small grains. Peaches produced 'old peach', and 'peray' was a liquor made from pears. Apple trees grew abundantly on the east coast, and applejack became a very popular drink.

Probably the most popular early distillery products were rum types, generally produced from molasses brought from the Caribbean, and by the mid eighteenth century there were more than sixty rum distilleries in Boston alone.

It is impossible to date accurately the first whiskey distilleries in America, but it is thought that colonial whiskey was produced in Pennsylvania in 1683, using pot-stills. Great expertise was brought to North America by the Irish and Scottish immigrants, well versed in the art of distilling, who arrived in the years following the Ulster Potato Blight of 1716–17. The immigrants settled first in Massachusetts, where they distilled their *usque baugh*, the production of which became a way of life for many of the new colonists. Whiskey could of course be produced by even a small farmer who grew grain and was able to construct a pot-still. The making of pot-still whiskeys was a natural phase of farming for the new immigrants. One of the most famous distillers of the time was George Washington, whose Mount Vernon distillery was managed by a Scotsman, James Anderson. The quality of this whiskey was highly regarded throughout the colonies.

As time went on, the early settlers began moving west, first into the western section of Pennsylvania and then beyond. The wilderness of the new land was turned into productive farms where huge crops of rye and corn were grown. The new territories were of course roadless, so that most trade was conducted by using pack-horses. The cost of transporting a barrel of flour made from grain exceeded its value on the eastern market, and the farmers were quick to realize that if the grain were converted to whiskey, a horse could carry six times the equivalent of grain in liquid form; furthermore, whereas the quality of the grain would have deteriorated the quality of the whiskey increased with age and movement. Vitally important to the farmer also was the fact that the value of the whiskey was much more stable than the fluctuating prices of the raw material. At that time Maryland and Pennsylvania produced mainly rye whiskey, whereas Virginia and Kentucky produced corn whiskey.

Virtually every settler in the new territories went into the whiskey distilling business, and every farm produced its own rye and grain whiskeys during the long winter months after the harvest.

In 1791 the newly formed United States were desperately in need of revenue and imposed a tax of 54 cents per gallon on the capacity of every still and a 7 cents per gallon tax on each gallon of whiskey produced. The Secretary of the Treasury decreed that the tax be paid in cash and arranged for Revenue Officers to be assigned to every district to ensure collection of the tax. Expectedly the reaction to this tax was extremely violent, and feelings ran high; Revenue Officers were tarred and feathered. Distillers who paid their taxes were called traitors, and committees were formed to find ways of fighting the tax. The situation became so explosive that in the autumn of 1794 a large army was necessary to put down the whiskey rebellion. The result of the rebellion was the movement west of many Pennsylvanian farmers, unhappy about the whiskey tax, who took their stills and other belongings and travelled down the Ohio River to Kentucky in the hope that they would elude the Revenue Collectors; but eventually the farmers registered their stills and paid their taxes.

The new Kentucky lands were originally planted with traditional rye, but it was found that the soil was far better suited to the growing of corn. The early settlers had, of course, been experimenting with distilling whiskeys made from various grains, looking for the perfect combination with the richness of rye and the smoothness of corn.

Historically, the Rev. Elija Craig is credited with producing the perfect whiskey, supposedly by accident, in 1789. Craig found the ideal combination of corn, rye, barley, malt and other grains, and he is also credited with the invention of Bourbon. According to legend, Craig one day was heating his white oak staves for making barrels. He was called away from his labours and upon his return found that some of the staves had become charred. He used these charred staves in making one of the barrels and, later, to his astonishment, found that the whiskey stored in this particular barrel was the best of the batch. Craig operated in what was then part of Kentucky's Bourbon country and his newly invented drink was named Kentucky Bourbon, particularly to distinguish it from Pennsylvania Rye.

The choice of Kentucky as the location of the distilleries for making Bourbon was more than a geographical accident. A huge limestone shelf runs under northern Kentucky and extends into southern Indiana and northern Tennessee, and through the limestone run fresh-water springs, completely free of iron and other minerals that could spoil the taste of whiskey. When the original distillers moved into Kentucky, the pure cold water tumbling down the hillsides was essential for cooling the distillates and also in the original making, and even today the main distilling centres in the U.S.A. are located in areas where water is obtained from natural springs that emerge through limestone rock.

The modern American definition of whiskey is 'an alcoholic distillate from a fermented mash of grain, produced at less than 190 U.S. proof (95° alcohol) in such a manner that the distillate possess a taste, aroma and characteristic generally attributed to whiskey stored in oak containers (except corn whiskey which need not be so stored) and bottled at not less than 80 U.S. proof, also includes the mixtures of such distillates for which no specific standards of identity are prescribed. Bourbon, rye, wheat, malt or rye malt whiskey are whiskies produced at not exceeding 160 U.S. proof, fermented mash are 51 per cent corn, rye, wheat, malted barley or malted rye grain respectively and stored at not more than 125 U.S. proof in charred, new oak containers and also include mixtures of such whiskies of the same type.'

The law until recently insisted on new charred oak casks being used for storage, but now used casks are permitted, much to the disappointment of distillers in Scotland, who imported them and may now have difficulty in obtaining casks. The purpose of using burnt casks is to mellow the taste and aroma and to impart colour. Many American whiskeys are labelled 'Bottled in Bond', which does not have the same meaning as in the United Kingdom. Obviously the whiskey is bottled under government supervision, but these whiskeys have extra stipulations that the strength may not be less than 100 U.S. proof, except for export at not less than 80 proof, the whiskey must be at least four years old, and it must be distilled spirits of the same kind, produced by the same distiller at the same distillery in the same distilling season. For these bonded whiskeys, the Government Tax Strip is green for domestic and blue for export, whereas it is red for other whiskeys.

American Light Whiskey

The new four-year-old American light whiskey was allowed to be sold on 1 July 1972. It is strictly defined (25 January 1968) in the following terms: 'Light Whiskey is whiskey which has been distilled in the U.S.A. more than 160 U.S. proof, stored in used or un-charred new oak containers and bottled at not less than 80 U.S. proof and also includes mixtures of such whiskies. If light whiskey is mixed with the mixture it shall be designated "Blended Light Whiskey".'

The introduction of a light whiskey was intended by American distillers to combat the ever increasing sales of the lighter styles of Scotch whisky and therefore to reduce the volume of imports. At the time that light whiskey was defined, senior representatives of leading distilleries made statements which, in view of lack of enthusiasm for the product, are interesting as demonstrating that the crystal-ball-gazing marketing executives are not infallible and cannot always 'get their sums right'. 'The laying down of stocks of light whiskey involves a sizeable investment in an unknown product; it is a tremendous gamble . . .', 'We simply have no idea what the American public's reaction to light whiskey will be.'

The attempt to produce a new style of whiskey with the tremendous financial advantages of distillation at high strength and efficiency, the use of old casks and of being able to state the age of a whiskey has not proved to be successful. To the question, 'Why introduce a new product to already overcrowded shelves?' Mr Haefelin, who was largely responsible for Federal approval for the light whiskey idea, replied: 'The answer lies with the consumer; he and especially she are buying more lightly flavoured Canadian and Scotch Whiskies, low flavour rums and flavourless Vodka than ever before.' At the time of first availability a spokesman for the distilled spirit industry said: 'It is a general consensus of opinion in the trade that the new whiskey will not enlarge the overall market.' While light whiskey has not sold well as such, large quantities are used in place of the neutral spirit component in some blended whiskeys.

Canadian Whiskey

Rye-flavoured blended whiskeys distilled in Canada similarly to methods used for the best Kentucky Bourbon. Different flavours are produced by variation of the cereal proportions. The Canadian Whiskeys are mild and full of character.

American Whiskey Terms

Sour Mash is a term frequently used which refers to the natural fermentation of the yeast and the grain where dealcoholized ferment from a previous distillation has been added to the mash. The process gives continuity of character and reinforces the flavour and bouquet.

Straight Whiskey is pure whiskey (Bourbon, Rye, Corn) to which only pure water is added to reduce to the correct strength. The grain mixture must contain at least 51 per cent of the type which gives the whiskey its character and name.

Moonshine   Illicitly distilled whiskey drunk strong and rough.

WELSH WHISKY

Although whisky is no longer distilled in Wales it is interesting to record that a distillery was built in Bala in 1887, with the intention of producing sufficient whisky for distribution throughout Great Britain.

However, even using Scots and Irish expertise the venture proved unsuccessful and only the memory of the whisky remains together with the optimistic tone of its advertising: 'Welsh whisky is the most wonderful which ever drove the skeleton from the feast, or the painted landscapes in the brain of man. In it you will find the breath of June, the carol of the lark, the dew at night, the wealth of summer, autumn's rich content, all golden within imprisoned light.'

A new Welsh distillery is currently being planned for production of whisky, gin and vodka.

JAPANESE WHISKEY

Considerable progress has been made by the Japanese in popularizing their own whiskey distillations, which very often contain a large proportion of Scotch malt whiskies to enrich the flavour. Investment in the Japanese whiskey distilleries is large and major brands such as Suntory and Nikka have become very popular in their home market and will, no doubt, be marketed in other countries in due course. It is interesting to record that even with their copying expertise the Japanese have failed to imitate perfectly the original Scotch whiskies and notwithstanding local competition, the demand for Scotch continues to grow in Japan.

5
Gin

The production of spirit flavoured with juniper berries has been known for four hundred years and originated in Holland. It is said that a Dutch apothecary, Sylvius of Leyden, first experimented with juniper berries in wine and then turned to spirits, calling his product 'genievre'—gin to us, geneva or genever to Continentals. It was originally produced for purely medical reasons, the juniper being of diuretic value in flushing the urinary system, and the alcohol, of course, acting as a stimulant.

British soldiers returning from the Continent introduced gin to England and when William of Orange, who banned French imports and encouraged the use of English grain for distilling, became King in 1689, he encouraged the distillation of gin to counter the smuggling of French brandy. One of the very first Acts of the new reign was 'An Act for encouraging the consumption of malted corn and for the better preventing of French and Foreign Brandy'. There is no possible doubt about the complete and disastrous success of this Act. At no other period of history did the masses respond more enthusiastically to the call of patriotism as when they were called upon to be patriotically drunk. Nor can one wonder at the increase of drunkenness, with its attendant misery and wretchedness so well depicted by Hogarth, that followed such a policy. It was then that a Southwark inn dared put up a sign:

Drunk for 1d.
Dead drunk for 2d.
Clean straw for nothing.

And yet, apparently anxious to accelerate the rate of demoralization of the gin-sodden populace, Queen Anne's ministers removed the one safeguard which still prevented the worst kinds of spirits from being distilled in England: they cancelled the privilege of the Distillers' Company, a privilege which carried with it strict duties as to apprenticeship and a certain control over English distilleries. Henceforth the unscrupulous were free from all supervision.

The popularity of gin spread rapidly; it is estimated that by 1690 consumption was about half a million gallons and that by 1727 this had risen to 5 million gallons, when the total population of the country was only about 6½ million. During the period much illicit spirit also was sold, the impracticable and unenforceable Gin Act, designed to control the spirit trade, encouraging its distillation. The remedy proposed was too drastic to be effective: by the Act of 1736, gin was to be taxed so much that it would be beyond the means of the masses, and its sale in small quantities was prohibited.

The Gin Act of 1736 gave rise to disturbances, and even riots to begin with, and although it was not repealed until 1743, it could not have been enforced strictly, if at all, since the excise receipts show that in 1714 2 million gallons of gin were distilled in London, in 1733 11 million and in 1742 20 million gallons when it was estimated that there must have been not less than 400,000 dram-drinkers in London and within a radius of ten miles. At that time a historian wrote: 'The passion for gin seems to have infected the masses of the population and it spread with the rapidity and violence of an epidemic.' In 1751 An Address to an Eminent Person upon an Important Subject was sent to the Prime Minister by the Bishops and the College of Physicians, who asked that the duty on spirits be drastically increased, and that the penalties for all licensing offences be severely applied, adding: 'If all this be not found to answer the end, as distilled spirits are no necessaries of life, in the name of God, let the art be condemned as unlawful, let all spirituous liquors be seized and destroyed, wherever found, and the Commonwealth saved at any rate.'

The duty on spirits was then raised to 7 guineas per tun, and in 1756 the distillation of corn in England was prohibited altogether, owing to the failure of the harvest at home, and 'to encourage the importation of rum from the Colonies'. This prohibition, which does not appear to have been very effective, was repealed in 1760, when a further duty of £24 10s per tun was levied on all home-made corn spirits, and, ever since, the legislators have had recourse to increased taxation for the dual purpose of checking excessive drinking and filling the treasury coffers.

At that time, most of the gin drinkers were town and city workers, and not infrequently gin was given in lieu of wages. In the mid eighteenth century there were over seven thousand 'grog' shops in London, and with the growth of the cities with the Industrial Revolution, new drinking houses, the gin palaces, were built. Gladstone in 1871 tried unsuccessfully to control the number of public houses; gin was blamed entirely for insobriety.

Gin had a slow road to respectability. The upper classes despised the drink as being a tipple of the mob, as shown in several Hogarth canvases. There were of course supporters for gin; Lord Byron claimed that gin and water provided his inspiration. In the mid nineteenth century Dr Sigert in the South American town of Angostura developed his blend of aromatic and tonic bitters which were an obligatory medicine at the time in the Royal Navy, when it was discovered that the addition of gin to these bitters produced a most palatable beverage. These bitters, originally prepared for medicinal use, were soon being exported all over the world as flavouring for spirits.

Similarly, in the outposts of the Empire, where quinine water or quinine-flavoured tonic was an essential drink for health reasons, it was found that the addition of gin produced a most delectable mixture, and the gin and tonic gained popularity as retired soldiers and administrators returned home from the East.

The London Dry Gin was introduced a century ago as an unsweetened variety in total contrast to the Dutch style, and this has continued to be the most popular. Gin has maintained its position, although the increasing sales of vodka with its freedom from taste has had an effect on demand. You can still hear gin referred to as Mother's ruin—perhaps a reference to the myth that juniper berries act as an abortifacient.

The introduction of the continuous still by Coffey in 1831 allowed the production of gin to be based on pure spirit, and the distillers improved the quality of their product enormously. As the product improved, it began to be enjoyed by higher social levels, and of course in the twentieth century it has been totally accepted as one of the classic spirits of the world.

Gin is produced from neutral grain spirit with the addition not only of juniper, but of other 'botanicals', such as coriander, angelica, caraway, aniseed, orange peel, cardamom, calamus root, cassia bark, orris root, liquorice root and dozens more, each distiller having his own secret formula not only of mixture proportions, but also of the exact origin of the herbs and spices.

There are three very important basic essentials which contribute to the character of gin: rectified spirit, which must be totally free from impurities; the variety of 'botanicals', which is entirely the distiller's choice; and the design and control of the still. The neutral spirit is usually distilled a second time after reduction in strength to 60 per cent alcohol. It is of course essential for the spirit to be clean and tasteless, and most gin spirit is produced in patent stills from grain. (Spirit from other sources such as potatoes is used in some European countries to make vodka.)

Either the botanicals are added to the spirit, which is then distilled and a definite fraction of the distillate collected, or vapour extraction methods are used. This is through a 'gin head' where spirit vapour passes through a layer of botanicals, extracting flavouring en route, selected fractions of distillate again being separated.

The art of the gin distiller is the control of the rate of distillation and in the examination of the part of the distillate which is suitable for the gin he is producing. The first stage of the distillation, the head, is not used, and the distillate is collected in a feints receiver. When the distillate has the required flavour, the output is then run into a gin receiver. Control over the quality is a combination of sampling for alcoholic strength and nosing for flavour content. As the distillation proceeds, these qualities change, and the distiller must most carefully determine the point of cut-off. The last part of the distillation is the tail, which is also collected in the feints receiver, the feints being re-used later.

In 1969 a United States definition for potable spirits for sale in the U.S.A. defined gin as 'a product obtained by original distillation from mash or re-distillation of distilled spirits or by mixing neutral spirits with or without juniper berries and other aromatics or with or over extracts derived from infusions, percolations or macerations of such materials and include mixtures of gin and neutral spirit. It shall derive its main characteristic flavour from juniper berries and be bottled at not less than 80 U.S. proof.'

Gin is not usually matured before marketing and does not carry any age certificate. The difference in taste between gins is a combination of factors—the distillation technique, the mixture of botanicals, and the quality of the spirit.

Flavoured Gins

Most flavoured gins are produced by steeping the selected fruit in gin; artificial or extracted flavour compounds can be used but are, of course, second best. Orange and lemon gins are still produced, mainly for export markets. Dutch distillers also produce flavoured gins which are popular in the Netherlands; blackcurrant gin is currently available in the United Kingdom.

London Gin

Originally this was dry gin produced in or near London, but nowadays there is no geographical significance to the term London. Most modern British and American gins are dry and very similar.

Plymouth Gin

Plymouth gin is a heavier, more strongly flavoured gin than the London dry type. It is the popular Royal Navy drink; pink gin is made from Plymouth gin and angostura bitters.

Dutch Gin (Holland's, Genever or Schiedam)

All Dutch distilleries produce Holland's gin, which has a fuller and riper flavour than British or American gins. Although the same botanicals are used (in different proportions, of course), it is the nature of the spirit which gives the taste variation and particular character. The spirit is not completely tasteless neutral grain, but spirit that has been distilled in a pot-still from a mash containing a large proportion of malt, which on distillation there-fore produces some congeners normally associated with whisky. The 'beer' produced from the cereal mash fermentation is distilled in a pot-still and re-distilled at least once, with distillate collected at less than 60 per cent alcohol. Some genevers were quadruple distilled. Finally, the spirit is re-distilled with a mixture of botanicals (mainly juniper berries), which gives it a characteristic flavour. The genever is called Jong. A second type, Oud, is Jong genever compounded with distilled grape products, possibly other flavours, and may be slightly coloured. The Dutch also produce flavoured genevers which appear to be popular only in Holland.

Dutch gins are distilled at lower alcoholic strength than British types. It is said that the term 'Dutch Courage' originated with English soldiers fighting in Europe, who fortified themselves with this very warming drink.

Wacholder is a German gin similarly manufactured.

Steinhäger

German gin is produced in Westphalia. Marketed in tall stone flagons, it is colourless with a distinct juniper flavour. Production is by distillation of fermented juniper berries. Extra juniper berries may be added to the distillate to increase the flavour.

Similar production methods are used for Borovicka (Slovakia), Kranawitter (Tyrol) and Klekowatsch (Balkans).

Golden Cock Gin

Norwegian gin reputedly very smooth.

Old Tom Gin

Slightly sweetened London gin popular in colder climates. The name is credited to a Captain Bradstreet, who is said to have nailed the sign of a cat to his London house, and with a tube served gin through the cat's paw! Payment was through the cat's mouth. The original gin sling was 'Tom Collins', made from Old Tom gin, while 'John Collins' was made with London gin.

Pimms No. 1 Gin Sling

A flavoured gin-based speciality drink designed to be served as a long drink by dilution with sparkling lemonade. Pimms No. 2–6, no longer produced, were based on whisky, brandy, rum, rye whiskey and vodka, respectively.

6
Vodka

Vodka is an original eastern European beverage, and although it is thought of as the Russian national drink, it is believed by some authorities to have a Polish background.

Vodka, or *wodka*, means 'little water' and appears to have been known for eight centuries. The records mention that Russian vodka was first distilled in the twelfth century mainly for medicinal purposes, usually from the cheapest local agricultural produce, wheat, rye, maize, potatoes, sugarbeet, etc. The Poles, however, argue that they were the first *wodka* producers. Distilleries appeared in neighbouring east European countries, and vodka became popular, especially in the colder northern regions. It is, regrettably, impossible to trace the exact origins.

European vodka is spirit obtained from potato (although grain spirit is now used in reproducing old vodka types) and, after a second pot-still distillation, is filtered through charcoal, which removes all flavour and bouquet characteristics. The spirit, which has a remarkable smoothness, is not normally aged, although some vodka produced in Holland is matured for at least five years in wood. As with all spirits, the quality is largely dependent upon the nature of the base spirit and the water used in diluting the high-strength spirit. With flavoured vodkas, of course, wood maturing adds smoothness of flavour.

Serious vodka production began in western Europe when Russian and Polish émigrés fled after the Revolution. Vodka drinking began seriously in the U.S.A. at the beginning of the Second World War, when Hueblein bought Smirnoff Vodka and heavily promoted it. Vodka has been acknowledged by the Americans officially and can be defined as 'neutral spirits so distilled or so treated after distillation with charcoal or other materials as to be without distinctive character, aroma, taste or colour'. The success of vodka in America is shown by the increase of consumption from 386,000 gallons in 1950 to 86,000,000 gallons in 1975.

The vodkas produced in Great Britain and the U.S.A. are fairly tasteless, neutral, highly rectified grain spirit whose main virtue is that in mixed drinks the spirit can be 'felt but not smelt', a far cry from the original eastern European vodkas with characteristic flavour, which are enjoyable on their own. Russian vodka is said to be the Petrovskaya type based on a seventeenth-century formula invented by Peter the Great. All spirit production is now in the hands of the Russian State monopoly, Prodintorg.

The fashion for vodka mixes came out of California, and has gradually spread eastward, back whence vodka originated. Statistics show that sales of British and American types of vodka are steadily increasing, and will continue to do so for the spirit 'that leaves you breathless'.

Vodka was introduced to England about eighty years ago, when Maurice Meyer imported Riga Wodka from the House of Wolfschmidt. Before the Second World War, when supplies from Latvia ceased, the Riga formula was reproduced in Holland and sold under the brand of 'Nicholoff', after long maturing in cask. In the last decade, vodka has become one of the most widely marketed spirits, much of its popularity coming from its neutral flavour which makes it very suitable for mixed drinks. It is a superb drink with smoked fish when it is taken neat. Many *hors d'oeuvre* dishes prove unsuitable for wine drinking, but the perfect accompaniment is provided by vodka, especially the Dutch, the Polish Vyborowa or Wyborowa types and Russian Stolichnaya types. High-strength vodkas are imported from Russia (Krepkaya, 56 per cent), and Poland (80 per cent white spirit neutral vodka); the western brand leader, Smirnoff, is also available at high strength (43 per cent).

Many flavoured vodkas are now produced in Poland and Russia, among them:

Subrowka (Zubrowka). Polish vodka flavoured by steeping Zubrowka grass (bison grass), resulting in a spirit with a delicate aromatic bouquet. The specially shaped bottle usually contains a

stem of the grass. Because of the colour from the grass, it is sometimes known as green vodka.

Starka. Old Russian vodka prepared from an infusion of leaves
of Crimean apple and pear varieties, plus a dash of brandy and
port-type wine. The vodka is mellow with a pleasing bouquet with
a hint of wine flavour.

Polish Starka is high-strength vodka aged in wood; Krakus is a
specially fine quality vodka; Winiak is golden brown 43 per cent
Polish vodka matured in wine casks for five years.

Yubileynaya Osobaya (Jubilee Vodka). A vodka introduced in 1957
containing Cognac, honey and other ingredients.

Pertsovka (Pepper Vodka). A dark brown Russian pepper vodka
with a pleasing aroma and burning taste, said to be good in
treating stomach disorders. It is prepared from an infusion of
capsicum, cayenne and cubeb.

7
Calvados

~~~~~~

This is apple brandy, which takes its name from Calvados, the Normandy centre, ideal, with its damp climate, for the French apple orchards. It is a beautiful liquid with glints of amber, a potent yet delicate fragrance. Calvados, with its irreplaceable flavour, contributed very early to the renown of the gastronomy of Normandy.

Centuries ago Norman and Breton peasants made a primitive drink from apples which grew wild in the local forests. By the eighth century Charlemagne, in his *De Villis*, was instructing his stewards to plant orchards, and the first rules were established for making cider. Calvados is romantically linked with the Vikings. When the Norsemen took over Normandy over a thousand years ago, they found rich farmlands and apple orchards and soon discovered the pleasures of apple alcohol.

In 1553 it is recorded that Gilles de Gouberville, agronomist and gastronome, distilled for the first time 'eau-de-vie de cidre', or cider spirit, in the little village of Mesnil-au-Val, now in Manche.

The North American settlers also enjoyed their fruit spirits. Robert Beverly in his *History of Virginia*, 1722, gives a most informative destription of the horticultural and distillation practices involved in this domestic production:

'The Fruit Trees [apples] are wonderfully quick of Growth; so that in six or seven years time from the Planting, a Man may bring an Orchard to bear in great Plenty, from which he may make Store of good Cyder, or distill great Quantities of Brandy; for the Cyder is very strong, and yields abundance of Spirit . . . [Peaches] commonly bear in three Years from the Stone . . . others make a Drink of them, which they call Mobby, and either drink it as

Cyder, or distill it off for Brandy. This makes the best Spirit next to Grapes.'

New Jersey was also the centre at a very early date for distilling apple whiskey, whose potency is suggested in the name Jersey Lightning, so called because it struck suddenly and produced an affliction known as 'apple palsy'.

Early types of Calvados were made in glass stills surrounded by stones heated by wood fires. Later, copper stills were introduced, and since then designs have remained very similar to present-day 'Charentais' (Cognac) stills.

Imitators rapidly appeared, and by 1757 there were enough Norman distillers for them to form a corporation to protect their interests. Some of the names on the original list of members are still well known today: Bunel, Desjonqueres and Leblanc.

In 1588 Philip II of Spain sent a fleet of 130 ships to Britain to avenge the death of Mary, Queen of Scots, and overthrow Elizabeth; it was the 'Invincible Armada'. But there was no landing, for the English attacks sank or scattered the Spanish vessels, one of which, the *Calvador*, ran aground on the reefs off the French Channel coast. Those reefs were then called after the ship, and the name was later applied to the *département*; since much cider was distilled in this district, the brandy then obtained finally took the name of 'Calvados'. It was not until the early nineteenth century, however, that cider spirit made in Normandy took the name Calvados.

Legend has it that the Normans enjoyed a glass of Calvados in the middle of a meal, which not only facilitated digestion, but also sharpened the appetite for greater enjoyment of the remainder of the repast. Such enjoyable customs are, of course, handed down from generation to generation, and this one became known as the 'Trou Normand'—the Norman hole making space for further food. As an appetizer, Calvados should be tossed back in one gulp; as a brandy or apéritif 'on-the-rocks' it should be slowly sipped.

Fully ripe apples are crushed and fermented with cultured yeast and the mash is pot-distilled to produce low wines, which are then re-distilled to produce Calvados of high strength. Maturing in oak casks is essential; 'Un Trou Normand', one of the finest, is at least six years old before it is bottled and is golden brown, the colour obtained from its slow maturing in the casks. All Calvados improves with ageing in oak casks.

All Calvados must be submitted to a tasting committee. Before a Certificate of Quality is granted allowing the brandy sample to be called 'Calvados', it must pass the scrutiny of experts, who jealously guard the reputation of their Normandy brandy.

All aspects of Calvados production are strictly controlled, both by the authorities and by the producers and dealers themselves. Since 1942 the Institut National des Appellations d'Origine has recognized three distinct qualities of cider-based spirits:

(1) 'Le Calvados-Pays d'Auge'—Appellation Contrôlée—made in Charentais-type stills.

(2) 'Le Calvados'—Appellation Réglementée—made in open fire stills.

(3) 'Eau-de-vie de cidre'—Appellation Réglementée—made with vapour columns.

The regulations stipulate that Calvados must be made from apples or pears harvested in, and ciders or perries distilled on, the whole of the production area claiming the appellation of origin of: 'Calvados du Pays d'Auge', 'Calvados de L'Avranchin', 'Calvados du Calvados', 'Calvados du Cotentin', 'Calvados du Domfrontais', 'Calvados du Mortanais', 'Calvados du Pays de Bray', 'Calvados du Pays de la Risle', 'Calvados de la Vallée de L'Orne', 'Calvados du Pays de Merlerault' and 'Calvados du Perche'. It must be made from ciders or perries obtained by milling the fruits, by crushing or grating or separating the juices obtained by draining alone, or by extracting the juice by either an intermittent or a continuous extraction press. The extraction of the juice may be facilitated by macerating the pulp in water. The fermentation of the juice must have taken place naturally at least one month before extraction.

This brandy must be distilled by means of so-called 'Charentais' double distilling or continuous or intermittent primary flow stills allowing for the elimination of first and last runnings.

Calvados, Appellation Réglementée, is generally obtained by single distillation of ciders from specific delineated areas. To ensure highest quality, the regulations specify a maximum speed of distillation.

Calvados du Pays d'Auge, Appellation Contrôlée, can be distilled only from ciders originating in a privileged zone 'Pays d'Auge', where extremely high-grade fruit is produced. Two distillations from copper Charentais stills are necessary. The first distillation produces *petites eaux* (*brouillis*) at between 20 and 30 per cent alcohol which are re-distilled, the 'heads and tails' being put aside and only the main central distillation qualifying for the Appellation.

In the U.S.A., 'applejack' is made similarly, but it is generally marketed younger than is Calvados.

Special designations are rarely used for Calvados but are permitted as follows:

3 Star *or* 3 Apples,	minimum age 2 years
Vieux *or* Réserve	minimum age 3 years
V.O. *or* Vieille Réserve	minimum age four years
V.S.O.P.	minimum age 5 years
Napoleon *or* Hors D'Age	
or Age Inconnu	minimum over 5 years

8
Brandy

~~~~~~~~~~~~~~~

Brandy is the spirit distilled from fermented fruit juice (fruit wine) and is the anglicized form of the Dutch *Brantjwyn*, the German *Branntwein* and *Weinbrand*, meaning 'burnt wine'. The French call it *eau-de-vie-de-vin*.

Spirits are drinks composed principally of ethyl alcohol obtained from the fermentation and subsequent distillation of a plant or fruit and containing a series of secondary substances of various kinds which give each type of spirit its characteristic bouquet. French brandy, *eau-de-vie*, however, is coloured (and thus lightly flavoured) agricultural spirit, whereas grape brandy, *eau-de-vie-de-vin*, is distilled wine.

The generic term brandy as used in England is taken to mean grape brandy—the product obtained by the distillation of grape wine. Some wines, of course, are better suited for distillation than others; the best, from a small, strictly limited area in south-west France, are entitled to the name of Cognac, which calls for a chapter to itself.

Grape brandies are made in all wine-producing countries, and those from France, Italy, Greece, Cyprus, Spain, Australia, Israel, the U.S.A. (some of which is produced in continuous stills giving spirit of more uniform quality than that produced by pot-still distillation) and the Iron Curtain countries, are well known and are naturally used in liqueur production. German brandy is not usually distilled from German wine but from other European wines which are less expensive. In France brandy distilled from wine from specified areas can be called 'Fine de . . . Bourgogne, etc.' (from Burgundy, etc.).

EAU-DE-VIE DE MARCS

Brandy distilled from the fermented pulpy residues after the pressing of grapes for wine is made in most French wine districts. Distillation is usually performed in the village square in a mobile still which is transported from village to village. It is called *grappa* in Italy and *Tresterschnapps* in Germany. Many years' maturing are required to smooth the fiery flavour. The recommended method of drinking it is to dip a sugar cube into the marc and suck the spirit out! It is often named after the district of origin: thus 'Marc de Bourgogne' is made from residues of Burgundy pressings.

Marc is made in the following areas of France: Aquitaine, Bourgogne, Bugey, Côteaux de la Loire, Champagne, Franche-Comté, Languedoc, Provence, Côtes du Rhône, Auvergne, Centre-Est, Savoie, Alsace (particularly Gewürztraminer).

Wine Spirits ('*Fine*') are brandies distilled from wine lees or wine and are usually less inflammatory products. They are made in many areas of France: Aquitaine, Bourgogne, Bugey, Côteaux de la Loire, Franche-Comté, Languedoc, Marne, Provence, Côtes du Rhône, Fougères.

Pisco is Peruvian brandy distilled from muscat wines. Similar products are made in other South American countries.

Fine de Bordeaux, introduced in 1974, is obtained exclusively by double distillation, in copper pot-stills, of Bordeaux wines. The distilled fine is matured in Limousin oak casks. Strict quality control is enforced and any lesser qualities are marketed as Eau de Vie d'Aquitaine.

Other Brandies. All wine-producing countries also produce brandies by either the pot-still or the continuous still process. These brandies are mainly for local consumption but exceptions are Italian, Spanish and Greek brandies, which have large export markets, as have those from South Africa and Israel.

9
Cognac

The delimited area for the production of wines for distilling into Cognac lies snugly in the basin of the River Charente to the north of the Gironde (about sixty miles north of Bordeaux), with the Cognac industry centralized on the towns of Cognac and Jarnac. The area is divided into seven sectors which were officially recognized by a law in 1909.

Grande Champagne, the finest of Cognacs, lies within the area of Cognac itself, and the vines in this area produce quality and quantity. The characteristics from this area are unusually fine quality, but require a long time in cask to obtain maturity.

Petite Champagne three-quarter surrounds the Grande Champagne area, and the Cognacs from this area are not dissimilar from those of the Grande Champagne, but generally have less body.

Borderies lies to the north-west of the Grande Champagne area and produces particularly mellow Cognacs.

Fins Bois completely surrounds the previous three areas; it produces excellent quality which matures more rapidly than the Grande and Petite Champagnes.

Bons Bois surrounds the Fins Bois, producing pleasant Cognacs, occasionally a 'goût du terroir'.

Bois Ordinaires and *Bois Communs* are the areas furthest to the north-west of the other growths, and Cognacs are produced here with a pronounced *goût du terroir*, supposedly due to the Atlantic climate and possibly to the use of seaweed as fertilizer.

Although distillation came to be practised in Cognac only in the early seventeenth century, the history of wine growing extends a

4. Map of Cognac

great deal further back in history. In the days of the Gauls, the area was noted for its wheat. The Romans introduced two additional sources of productive wealth, the cultivation of the vine and the extraction of salt along the Atlantic coast. The flourishing salt trade led to the establishment of the wine trade in the Middle Ages, as it was not unusual for wine to be despatched together with salt. The salt trade to northern Europe was particularly vital, and fourteenth-century records show that the wines also enjoyed an excellent reputation at that time.

In 1487 Charles d'Angoulême, the son of Jean-le-Bon, married Louise de Savoie. The young couple, light-hearted, joyful and carefree, made Cognac in a short space of time a brilliant artistic and intellectual centre. In 1492 their daughter Marguerite, the future Queen of Navarre, was born at Angoulême, and two years later, on 12 September 1494, their son François, later to become François I of France, came into the world at the Château de Cognac. Since Louis XII had no issue, François became the heir to the French throne. Once he became king, he never forgot Cognac and came there on several occasions with his family, his ministers, his suite and his mistresses. For these reasons, the château was completed, restored and embellished by him. In 1526 he signed, at Cognac, the Sainte Ligue, a treaty of alliance with Pope Clement VII, the Milanese and the Venetians. The object of this treaty was to counteract the plans of supremacy of the Emperor Charles V.

Cognac, which suffered a great deal from the Wars of Religion, opposing Protestant and Catholic troops, and also by the repeal of the Edict of Nantes, resumed an active economic life towards the end of the seventeenth century.

The distillation of wines from the Cognac area early in the seventeenth century was undoubtedly due to the recession in sales as a result of heavy taxation. Apparently the wines of that time did not travel too well, and deterioration occurred. Wine distillation had become widespread in France, mainly for the production of medicine, and during the sixteenth century it became a popular drink. The distillation of wines from the Cognac area produced brandy, which could be shipped to the old wine-importing countries without fear of deterioration. In 1619 the East India Company purchased some Coniak, in London, for their ships. Shipments were apparently at high strength as dilution took place on arrival. The northern countries which had purchased wines in the past now supported the distilled product, and by the beginning of the eighteenth century, brandy, or, as it was then known, Brandy Wine, completely replaced wine as the local export product. Not only had brandy replaced wine, but the brandy that was produced was found to have a most pleasant flavour and none of the undesirable tastes found in other brandies, which had to be covered by adding flavours. From the eighteenth century onwards Cognac was reputed to be the finest brandy in the world, and it was vital to the development of the area that the brandies improved enormously with age and could be stored without risk. It was in fact the need to warehouse the young spirit for long periods that inevitably turned the broker into a merchant, and these merchants, with their differing styles, produced by variation in blends from the areas within Cognac, eventually became the brands and famous Houses of Cognac that we know to this day.

How is this most wonderful of brandies produced?

For many white wines and all Cognacs the presence of chalk in the soil is an essential condition for a superb bouquet and high quality. A wine-loving chemist once wrote: 'From these soils wines of considerable bouquet are obtained.' The lime content of the soil and the bouquet of the wine obviously run parallel to each other.

The original vines of Cognac were completely destroyed by the ravages of *Phylloxera vastatrix*, and whereas most areas in France could find suitable American roots (which are phylloxera-resistant) for grafting the native vines on to, it was particularly difficult in the Cognac area because of the high chalk layer, and early attempts failed. The vines now planted in Cognac are grafted on to American rootstocks which are successful in this very difficult soil.

Happily, writers at the time of the replanting said that there was no perceptible change in the character of the Cognac, and from that time onwards the St Emilion vine gradually became the dominant variety for the area. The grafted St Emilion apparently proved better in so far as it is less sensitive to frosts and gives a larger yield, the grapes ripen earlier and are better in quality.

The very light wine is not regarded as a quality produce because it is high in acidity and low in alcohol, but this is very important in so far as the high natural acidity inhibits spoilage by micro-organisms, and the low level of alcohol means that a very high volume of wine is required to produce Cognac, so that there must be a positive enrichment in the flavouring compounds which are distilled. Until distillation, the wines are stored on their lees, and the wines are protected as far as possible from oxygen, which would alter the flavours of the wine and consequently of the brandy.

The chalky soil and this mild Aquitaine climate are ideal for the main variety of vine, the St Emilion Charente (the local name for the Ugni Blanc). The Colombard, which is native to this area, is also grown, as is the Folle Blanche. The grape varieties are detailed in a decree of May 1936.

After the harvest, vinification follows the normal procedure for white wine, except that the addition of sulphur dioxide is avoided, because it may harm the flavour and bouquet of the wine, which in turn are so vital for the flavour of the distillate. To the distiller, sulphur is an abomination, for his product is sensitive to every kind of nauseous odour and flavour, and merest traces could ruin it. The wine is distilled in the winter, immediately after fermentation and before it has been racked from the lees, for it is the lees that play so vital a part in producing the esters that form the characteristic bouquet of a good Cognac.

The final stage prior to bottling is the blending of various styles of Cognac and various ages of these styles to produce a standard product—standard, that is, for any particular shipping house. Generally Cognacs are lightly coloured with caramel, so that this standardization is perfect between various shipments.

The simple pot-stills for Cognac distillation are traditional in shape and general design. The onion-shaped pot-stills are in direct contact at the bottom with the fire from the hearth, and the vapours of the distillation are first passed through a special tank carrying cold wine which is about to be distilled, so that it is pre-warmed before its distillation (the pot is called *chauffe-vin*), economic both in time and cost.

The first important stage of the process is distillation to produce a low-strength product of approximately 29 per cent called *brouillis*. The pot-still distillation of *brouillis* is arranged to be slow and steady, and, as in all distillations, the first and last parts of the distillation are returned to the *brouillis*, and it is only the middle part of the distillation which is selected for maturing into Cognacs.

The vital main fraction of the distillation normally distils at 75 per cent alcohol by volume at the beginning of its collection, and the cut-off point is taken when the strength is reduced to

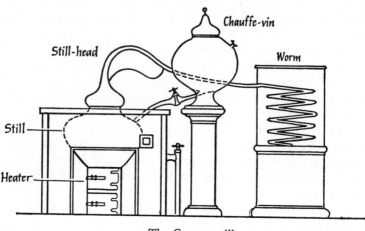

5. The Cognac still

between 60 per cent and 50 per cent at the end, so that the average strength is approximately 70–72 per cent. The quality of the Cognac is, in essence, controlled by the speed of the distillation, which is itself dependent upon the heat of the fire which boils the wine.

The result of the distillation is best considered as produced from soil, climate, vine, grower and distiller, but ultimately its future excellence depends on the quality of the casks and on time. The quality of the casks is absolutely vital. The oak casks that provide the ideal conditions for the maturing of Cognacs are traditionally from the Limousin and Troncias Forests. Before the casks are made, the wood is conditioned for many years in the open air, so that it dries and loses certain soluble extracts. The young Cognac takes colour from new wood and becomes darker as a result of the extraction of pigments and chemicals from the wood, and it is therefore essential to rack into older wood to prevent too much extraction of tannins and other soluble substances, such as polyphenols and aromatic aldehydes, taking place. Not much is known about the maturation process, but improvement in cask up to fifty years is considered normal. There is no doubt that the exposure to air within the cask causes slow oxidation of the various alcohols in the Cognac and that the resultant products combine in a very complicated and not altogether understood chemical reaction; perhaps the presence of some of the extracts from the wood produces a large range of esters which in combination with the alcohols and aldehydes produce the complicated mixture which we realize as bouquet. During storage of course a large quantity evaporates, and it is estimated that the equivalent of at least twelve million bottles of Cognac are lost every year 'to the Angels'.

The enjoyment of a great Cognac is in exactly the same order as that of a Claret or Burgundy. As the distilled quintessence of wine it is the perfect finale to a series of superb wines, and it stands alone and almost without rivals, although Armagnac can be mentioned in the same breath with it. Its special properties can be produced only by the distillation of the Charente wines which can be grown only in the Charente soil.

The mellowness and character of bottled Cognac depends a great deal on the skill of the blender in marrying the contents of many casks but also on the length of time the Cognacs have been stored in cask. Before bottling, Cognac may be lightly coloured with caramel. Once bottled, the spirit will not mature.

Cognacs are marketed with the name of either the French shipper or the importer, sometimes with additional brand names. Vintage declarations are usually not stated but are allowed. French-bottled Cognacs have authenticity controlled by the authorities in Cognac whereas Cognac shipped in cask must have the age substantiated by the importer. In the United Kingdom the landing date of Cognac in cask may be given if the cask is stored and the Cognac bottled in bond: 'Landed January 1960, bottled March 1975', a statement which can be checked with the records of H.M. Customs and Excise. This example would give the Cognac an age of fifteen years plus the age given on the original shipping document from Cognac.

Extra terminology is often given to Cognacs to assist marketing non-specific products:

V.S.O.   Very superior old
V.S.O.P.   Very superior old pale
V.V.S.O.P.   Very very superior old pale
X.O.   Extremely old

Fine Champagne: Cognac made from grapes grown in Grande and Petite Champagne areas (at least 50 per cent of the former).

Esprit de Cognac

This is never found as a marketed produce because it can only be used to 'liqueur' a sparkling wine or champagne. It is produced by a third distillation of Cognac and is, by law, high strength.

1980/81 Statistics

Cognac area: total	96,465 hectares
Grande Champagne	13,068 hectares
Petite Champagne	16,397 hectares
Borderies	4,194 hectares
Fins Bois	39,149 hectares
Bons Bois	20,159 hectares
Bois Ordinaires } Bois Communs }	3,498 hectares
Production	7,536,987 hectolitres of wine

10

Armagnac

Cognac has always been considered in Britain as the world's finest brandy, and it is seldom realized that Armagnac, the 'liquid gold of Gascony', was being distilled nearly two centuries before anyone had ever heard of Cognac. Legal documents in the archives of the Haute Garonne Department have references to 'ayga ardenterius' early in the fifteenth century; by the end of that century brandies were sold in the market of St-Sever (Landes). There is the delightful legend of Henry IV of France tasting Armagnac on the day of his birth. His grandfather is said to have moistened the lips of the child with Armagnac and a taste of garlic, from which he is said to have drawn 'wisdom and strength for his whole life'.

Armagnac is not of course to be directly compared with Cognac; they are both first-class brandies with individual characteristics and qualities. Old Armagnac is almost as much sought after as is old Cognac.

Armagnac brandy is entitled to that specific appellation only if it is distilled from wines produced within a strictly delimited geographical area. The wine used in its production can be derived only from specially nominated vines, and distillation must be under strictly defined conditions. The Armagnac so much enjoyed today retains the *goût du terroir*—a combination of soil and vine.

The production area of Armagnac is approximately a hundred miles south of Bordeaux and to the west of Toulouse in departments of Gers, part of Landes and part of Lot-et-Garonne. The whole Armagnac area is sub-divided into three distinctive areas of production: Bas Armagnac, Haut Armagnac and Ténarèze.

The main vine varieties planted are the Ugni Blanc, Blanquette Clariette, Colombard, Picquepoul, Plante de Graisse, Mauzac and

6. Map of Armagnac

Meslier. These vines thrive in very arable soil which is generally yellowish in colour and is a mixture of clay and fine sand. The climate is warm, sunny and freshened by sea breezes from the Atlantic. It is very important indeed for production of a fine brandy that the grapes are allowed to ripen, but not to over-ripen. The produce is harvested and vinified in the traditional white wine manner, except that the wine, as in Cognac, is produced without addition of sulphur dioxide, nor is it racked from its fermentation lees before distillation. Chaptalization is strictly forbidden. Distillation starts as soon as the wine has completed its fermentation and can be racked bright, and the year's production is normally distilled as fast as the plant in the distillery can manage.

To be entitled Appellation Contrôlée Armagnac, distillation of the wine can take place in only two types of still. The main Armagnac type of continuous still provides continuous feeding of wine, and it must have two or three superposed pots and functions without any rectifying device. An alternative method is double distillation by means of pot-stills.

After distillation the Armagnac is water-white, high strength, and contains congenerics that are the volatile constituents which give the brandy its taste. It is, however, essential to reduce the amount of these compounds and also to lower the alcoholic strength, and cask storage is therefore a vital part of the process. It is very important to select only the finest oak for the manufacture of casks, and for Armagnac it has been found that the wood from local forests is ideal for mellowing the new spirit, which may be left in cask for up to twenty years. During maturation, the casks are stored in dark cool cellars, and the Cellar Master uses all of his blending arts to ensure that, from a commercial point of view, a standard product is obtained for marketing. The deficiencies of one distillation are balanced with a specially good distillation; the fire of youth can be tempered with the smoothness of older spirit. The Armagnac is, of course, reduced in strength to the normal selling strength of 70 proof (40 per cent by volume), and this is achieved by reducing the strength of the spirit with a careful, step-by-step blending with distilled water.

Under French law the minimum age under which the terms Armagnac, Bas Armagnac and Ténarèze are allowed is effectively two years. For the designations V.S., V.O., V.S.O.P., or RÉSERVE to be used, five years must have passed from the original harvest, and the designations Extra, Napoleon or V.A. RÉSERVE need an additional year in cask. Armagnac has a special age rating based on 31 August of the year of the vintage being rated 0. The following year on 1 September it has a rating of 1 until the following 31 August, when on 1 September the rating becomes 2.

It is interesting to note that unblended Armagnacs may still be marketed with the vintage year of production shown on the label.

The production of Armagnac at present is much less than its

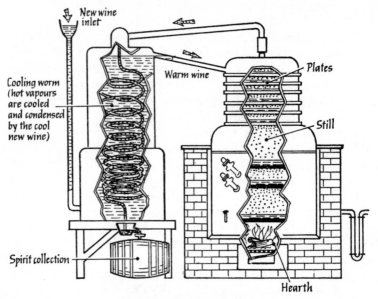

New wine inlet

Cooling worm (hot vapours are cooled and condensed by the cool new wine)

Warm wine

Plates

Still

Spirit collection

Hearth

7. The Armagnac still

potential, as only about half of the crop of approximately nine hundred thousand litres is distilled. It would therefore be fairly simple to double production, should the market growth demand this. It is unfortunate that such a fine product only has one-tenth of the brandy market in France and relatively small sales overseas, probably less than 5 per cent, and of this amount West Germany takes more than half. Consumption of Armagnac in the United Kingdom is relatively small, though a great deal of effort has been undertaken in the last few years to make Armagnac better known and more readily available, particularly in hotels and restaurants. In its very distinctive flagon shape bottle it is easy to recognize and, notwithstanding our very high excise duties, is normally slightly cheaper than Cognac.

Of the delimited area less than 10 per cent of the agricultural land is planted with vines. At the end of the last century phylloxera struck the Armagnac vineyards, which at the time covered 100,000 hectares, almost totally destroying all of the vines. Up to the Second World War the vineyards had been rebuilt to roughly half of their previous size, but since then the vineyard area has decreased to a low of 39,000 hectares in 1970; but further replanting in the following years has halted the slide. Generally the growers have smallholdings, and in the Bas Armagnac area two-thirds of these are between one and seven hectares. At present there are about 18,000 growers within the area, and about one-third of these belong to the Union de Co-operative Viticole d'Armagnac, which is a group of thirteen co-operatives whose production accounts for over 40 per cent of all Armagnac sales.

Armagnac is a particular favourite with fruit bottlers, and fruits bottled in Armagnac have proved very popular in most European countries where their sale is not hindered by excessive taxation.

Armagnac has been said to touch its zenith after twenty-five years, when it has extracted from the black oak staves of its cask all the goodness that it is possible for the wood to give.

It would be fair to conclude this chapter with a quotation from André Simon: 'Good Armagnac can be very good and much better than ordinary Cognac, but the best Armagnac cannot hope to approach, let alone rival, the best Cognac.'

1980/81 Statistics

Armagnac area: total	16,592 hectares
Bas Armagnac	9,449 hectares
Ténarèze	6,810 hectares
Haut Armagnac	333 hectares
Production	0·943 million hectolitres of wine

II
Tequila

Although Mexico is the land of the cactus, Tequila is in fact distilled from the fermented juice of the mezcal, otherwise known as the century plant. Producers say that it needs hot and dry ground to grow the mezcal, and production is centred specifically upon the small Mexican village of Tequila in the central Mexican state of Jalisco. The slopes surrounding the town of Tequila, amid the jagged Sierra Madre Occidental mountains, are pincushioned with the bluish-green variety of the argarth plant, which very much resembles an oversized pineapple, from which the Tequila is produced. The mezcal in fact looks like a very large spiked cactus which shoots enormous blossom spires into the sky. The bloom can take up to twelve years to produce.

It is widely believed that Tequila was the first spirit ever distilled in the New World and that the Aztecs discovered the secret of its production long before the first grain spirits were produced in America in the 1640s. The Mexicans apparently learned the secrets of the natural fermentation of the juice of the mezcal in approximately 300 B.C., and possibly the pre-Hispanic Indians included the wine in their religious ritual. The Spanish *conquistadores* in the early part of the seventeenth century found that the Aztecs had in fact been enjoying Tequila for generations, and its popularity in Mexico spread steadily. Surprisingly enough, it was only in the late 1950s that Americans travelling in Mexico brought their newly found enthusiasm for Tequila home, and now it is one of the most successful spirits sold on the North American market. The U.S. authorities have come to a reciprocal agreement and recognize that Tequila is solely a product of Mexico, and in return the Mexicans recognize that Bourbon whiskey is a distinctive product only of the U.S.A.

Tequila

The mezcal plant on maturity stands over 5 feet high and has a heart, or *pina*, which weighs at least 80 lb. Each *pina*, after processing, yields approximately 6 gallons of spirit.

The plants are stripped of their very graceful and pretty leaves, and only the hearts are sent to a distillery. The *pina* are there cut into chunks and the sweet juice is extracted by compression, steaming and washing. The mezcal juice is then fermented for three or four days, during which the sugars are converted into alcohol. The first distillation of this fermented mash produces a distillate of low strength, and the second distillation in the copper pot-stills produces Tequila at approximately 50 per cent alcohol. Tequila is of course pure white and only acquires its golden colour when it is matured in wooden casks. Although the market for Tequila in the United Kingdom is very small, it is interesting to note that in the U.S.A. importation in 1950 was approximately 12,000 gallons, and in 1981 it had risen to 7·4 million proof gallons.

The conventional method of enjoying Tequila is with salt and fresh lime juice; the juice is squeezed on the tongue, followed by a small amount of salt, and only then—Tequila. Its massive sales record in the U.S.A. has of course been achieved by the promotion of cocktails and mixed drinks (see Chapter 28).

Only the spirit distilled in or near the town of Tequila itself is entitled to be called Tequila. From other regions of Mexico the spirit is called Mezcal.

12

Rum

Rum is a generic term for a series of spirits produced from the fermented juice of sugar cane or molasses. Rums are produced in practically all sugar-growing countries. The name is believed to be derived from either of two words used in the West Indies in the seventeenth century—rumbullion and rumbustion—and it is thought that it originated in the East. The words were also current in Devon until quite recently. Alternatively the word may be derived from the Latin *saccharum*, meaning sugar, and the Dutch word *bulioen*, which means very precious metal. The famous rum and cola mixture can be traced back over a hundred years to Cuba, where white rums were used. During the Cuban struggle for independence at the end of the nineteenth century the insurgents took 'Viva Cuba Libre' as their rallying cry, and this gave rise to the name of the drink which encouraged them into action. The famous Daquiri Cocktail originates in Cuba, named after a former tin-mining town.

It is quite definite that rum was produced in the West Indies in the seventeenth century. In those days, the spirit was crude and drunk mainly by slaves; nowadays, with modern methods of production, rum has become a sophisticated drink which lends itself to numerous and very delicious mixed drinks.

Rum can be produced anywhere on the globe where sugar cane grows, but its home is in the Caribbean, and all of the islands are involved in its making, either commercially or perhaps in small pine-thatched shelters in the cane plantations in old illicit stills.

Historians have traced the use of cane sap in Chinese and Indian diets thousands of years B.C., and it is thought that the armies of Alexander in about 325 B.C. enabled this 'reed which gives honey without the help of bees' to reach the Mediterranean. The many sugar products obtained from cane sap tend to ferment spontaneously, giving an alcoholic beverage which, on distillation, gives a spirit—rum, which has been described by Father Labat as 'high alcohol giving strength to men and joy to women'.

In the late fifteenth century, Christopher Columbus introduced sugar cane to the Isle of Hispaniola, now the Dominican Republic and Haiti; the plants originated in the Canary Islands. Sugar cane was supposedly brought to Martinique in the early seventeenth century.

It is more than likely that the first spirituous liquor ever to be manufactured in America was made on Statten Island in a distillery established by Willem Keift, who was the Director-General of the New Netherlands. In 1664 the distillery was supposedly converted for the distillation of rum, although a rum distillery was operating in Boston as early as 1667, supplied with molasses by West Indian planters. A report of the time referring to Barbados says: 'The chief fuddling they make in the Island is Rum-Bullion, alias Kildevil, and this is made from sugar canes distilled, hot, hellish and terrible liquor.' The success of rum was instantaneous in North America and was to become New England's largest, most profitable and most unsavoury industry. The New England distillers became the central bankers of the slave trade, providing international currency for filling the vessels with slaves from the Guinea Coast, selling their slaves in the West Indies, in exchange buying molasses which were brought to New England and traded for another cargo of rum. The importance of New England rum continued until the prohibition of the importation of slaves in 1807, and was further diminished by the change in public preference to American whiskey.

In France the forerunners of rum were known as Tafias and Guildives, which compete with brandy. It was necessary to issue a royal decree in 1713 prohibiting the sale of molasses and extracts to protect the commerce in wine brandies, and it was not until 1763 that the king authorized his colonies to export rum to countries other than France, but only in exchange for products which could not be provided from France; eventually importation of rum from the French colonies was permitted, while prohibition of the import of other rums continued.

The rum trade in North America became so popular that by 1750 there were over sixty distilleries in Massachusetts and probably thirty on Rhode Island. Almost a thousand vessels were engaged in the slave trade route, and it is estimated that 12 million gallons of rum were being enjoyed each year. In 1733, however, Parliament in London passed the first Molasses Act in order to capitalize on the successful rum business, laying heavy duty on products from foreign islands into the New World colonies. Many believe that the troubles caused by this Act led to the American Revolution. The Molasses Act was so important because it resulted not only in the first of a series of outbursts against 'Taxation without Representation', but it also represented the first attempts to legislate social customs. Woodrow Wilson wrote: 'Out of cheap molasses of the French Islands, New England made the rum which was the chief source of her wealth. The rum with which she bought slaves from Maryland and the Carolinas paid her balances for the English Merchants.' The Act provided that only expensive molasses and rum from the British part of the West Indies could be imported into the Colonies duty free and that rums from the Dutch and French West Indies were subject to a prohibitive tax of 9d a gallon on rum and 6d a gallon on molasses. The 1763 Sugar Act slightly reduced the tariffs, but provided for very strict enforcements.

Among the more famous smugglers of the time were John Hancock and Samuel Adams, who were also deeply involved in the movement to break away from the British Crown.

Rum production is based on a standard procedure, with variations according to country. Freshly cut sugar cane is crushed to extract the juice which is then concentrated by boiling to a syrup. The sugar in the syrup is crystallized in a high-speed centrifuge, and the residual molasses are the basis for rum manufacture, which can be made as either light or heavy rums.

The French, however, until 1921 used to distinguish between the following:

Eau-de-vie de Canne, the spirit obtained by distillation of fermented sugar-cane juice (natural or slightly concentrated).

Le Rhum, the spirit obtained by distillation of fermented sugar cane juice to which had been added residues of previous distillations.

Le Tafia (Creole word), the spirit obtained by distillation of fermented molasses after extraction of the raw sugar.

LIGHT RUM — PUERTO RICO, CUBA, SOUTH AMERICA, ETC.

The molasses diluted with water and residues from the previous distillation are fermented with cultured yeast, and the resulting low alcoholic liquid is distilled in a column-still, so as to collect distillate of high strength (80 per cent alcohol), which results in a neutral-flavoured light rum, generally low in congeners. The important middle fraction only is matured in wood, and before bottling it is clarified and filtered through sand and charcoal. If the rum is to be sold dark in colour, caramel must be added, which ensures continuity of type.

FULL-BODIED RUM

(a) Jamaica Rum

The molasses are diluted with water and with the residues from the sugar boilers and fermented with natural yeast, assisted by residues from a previous fermentation. The weakly alcoholic solution is distilled in a pot-still and the resulting 'low wine' is redistilled, when the middle distillate fraction (produced at less than 80 per cent alcohol) is collected and matured in wood. The rum is usually coloured with caramel prior to bottling. The full-bodied rum is, of course, richer in congeners (giving a heavy pungent fullness) and requires longer than light rums to reach smoothness.

(b) Demerara Rum

As Jamaica rum, except that distillation is by column-still in place of pot-still.

VARIETIES

Jamaica. Jamaica is traditionally the home of heavy-bodied rums producing varieties that have a heavy pungent bouquet, body and flavour. The heavy types are known as Wedderburn and Plummer.

High-ester rums are produced by pot-still distillation where a very high yield of esters is aimed for. These rums are useful for blending with neutral (less expensive) spirits. Jamaica's best market is probably the United Kingdom, and rums are often shipped young for maturing in our own damp climate.

Guyana. Demerara, named after the local river near the sugar-cane plantations, is a most important rum, most of which is exported. Rapid fermentation techniques which emphasize a lightness of flavour are frequently employed and patent-stills are in use.

Trinidad produces medium light rums from continuous stills, rums that have excellent quality, but not depth of character.

Barbados. Pot and patent stills are used in distillation producing semi-light rums with a soft smoky flavour.

French rums. The French drink vast quantities of *rhum*, from the French West Indies, Martinique and Guadeloupe; also from Reunion Island in the Indian Ocean. Maturation and blending for the French market take place in France, mainly in Bordeaux and Le Havre. The rums tend to be fine and very rich in flavour, and are dark, fruity and Jamaican in style. The Martinique rums are made from cane juice. The Rhum St James is made by fermentation of a dunder with concentrated cane syrup and, like all heavy-style rums, is fermented slowly for from eight to twelve days. The results can be similar to the Wedderburn-style Jamaicans, and the very finest are called 'Grande Arôme'. Negrita, blended by Bardinet, is the brand leader in France and is produced in their 'Dillon' distillery. *Vintage* Dillon is marketed together with a range of rum cocktails, Daiquiri Planter's Punch and Coconut and also 'Old Nick' white rum.

The young rums are used to make the famous punch 'Martiniquais', which is probably an East Indian invention, the name deriving from the Hindustani *panch*, meaning five ingredients, originally tea, arrack, sugar, lemon and water, whereas the Martiniquais is usually made from rum, sugar and lemon peel.

Haiti. The influences in the distilling industry are totally French; double distillation occurs in pot-stills, as would be expected for the finest brandies. The first distillation product is clear white and called Clarin and is often used in Voodoo ceremonies.

Batavia arak, or arrack, is a brandy-like rum with strong flavour, distilled by the fermentation of molasses from the sugar factories near Batavia on the island of Java (see page 89).

Hawaii. Rum from these islands has recently been introduced to the United Kingdom and has a flavour between light and dark rums.

Puerto Rico, is the world's largest producer of rum by the patent-still method. These rums are dry and very similar to Cuban rums. Dark rums are also produced.

Cuba was well known in the past for very light rums, the original brands now being made in other areas, frequently Puerto Rico.

Quality variation between rums is due to natural factors such as the quality of the sugar cane, climate and soil, as well as to the method of distillation. The characteristic bouquet is in part due to bacterial action during fermentation, which causes some acetic acid formation.

Rum is a magnificent base for long mixed drinks, and large numbers have been recorded. The characteristic flavour allows a large proportion of diluting juice (fruit, soda, cola) to be used without loss of flavour. Some of the mixtures, known as punch, may have originated in the fortification of lime juice which was preserved for ships' stores by adding spirit to the juice. British sailors drank lime juice as protection against scurvy and obtained the nickname 'Limeys' from Americans. The British Customs manual still includes regulations for the fortification of lime and lemon juices.

Rum Verschnitt

A German blended spirit which contains at least 5 per cent rum, usually highly flavoured high-ether rum. 'Echter-Rum' is 100 per cent imported rum reduced with pure water to marketing strength.

13
Aquavit and Other Spirits

Aquavit, Akvavit (Scandinavian Spirit)

It has been said that 'if a man be bereft of speech in death, give him akvavit on his lips, and he shall at once regain his tongue'. Smørgåsbord, or smørrebord, and aquavit are ideal partners—the wonderful cold buffet and the cool, clear perfumed spirit of Scandinavia. Aquavit is certainly the national drink of Denmark, Sweden, Norway and Iceland and is made either from potato or grain spirit flavoured mainly with caraway, but also with citrus peel and herbs. Swedish aquavit has been sold for almost five centuries; some of it is made from potato spirit, which is rectified and charcoal filtered. Danish aquavit is generally considered the finest, and all Scandinavian spirits are produced under strictest government control. In Norway, Sweden and Iceland production is a government monopoly.

'Tafelaquavit' is very fine aquavit, where the spirit for distillation contains Kümmel, whose flavour is distilled into the final product.

The best-known brands are the Danish Aarlborg (which has been distilled in Aarlborg since 1846), Swedish O.P. Anderson, and Norwegian Gamel of Linie. The latter is a speciality spirit which is carried across the 'line' (equator) by Wilhelmsen liners on return voyages to Australia. The pale yellow colour comes from long maturing in American oak casks.

KORNBRANNTWEIN

German spirit made exclusively from Kornsprit (neutral spirit from mashed corn). The spirit may be flavoured, for example Wachholderkornbrannt, which is juniper-flavoured.

DOPPELKORN

As above, but at least 38 per cent alcohol.

FRUIT-FLAVOURED KORN

Apple, grapefruit, orange and pear Korn are very popular in Germany.

SNAPS, SCHNAPPS

Strong dry Dutch and German spirits which may be flavoured. In Scandinavia, the terms are generic and include aquavit.

Okelehao (Hawaiian Spirit)

'Oke' is produced by distillation in a column-still from the fermented mash of ti-plant roots. The distillate may be charcoal filtered before bottling. It is said to have an interesting and unusual flavour.

Ng Ka Py

Taiwan (Formosan) liqueur.

Mui Kwe Lu, Mow Toy Wine

High strength—43 and 51 per cent—spirits made from Kaoliang grain spirit, shipped to the United Kingdom from Hong Kong.

Arrak (East Indies Spirit)

The most famous is Indonesian, Batavia arrak from the Island of Java, best described as a brandy-like rum. The spirit is produced as a rum from molasses fermented with natural yeasts, including specially cooked rice in the mixture. Some Eastern manufacturers include coconut juice, or the juice of palm trees, in which case the distilled product is called 'toddy'. It is said that the combination of river water and natural yeast activity gives a special flavour which is very popular in Sweden, where the Batavia arrak is sweetened, flavoured and compounded into a liqueur called Arrack Punsch or Caloric Punsch.

Batavia arrak is usually wood-matured for several years. It is dry and highly pungent.

Most Eastern countries produce 'arrak' types, mainly from rice and sugar, but often including local fermentable produce. Many Mediterranean countries produce similar spirits which carry the generic title 'arrak' but bear little resemblance to the original Batavia arrak; they may be flavoured with local spices and are usually harsh and immature products.

In Sri Lanka, arrak is produced by double distillation in pot-stills of coconut toddy, followed by maturation in wooden vats.

Tiquira

High-strength Brazilian spirit obtained by distillation of malted and fermented tapioca roots.

Saké

Japanese rice wine is not a liqueur, although it is brewed to 30° proof by simultaneous processes which convert starch to sugar and then to alcohol. The ferments are Koji and Saké yeast. The distilled spirit is also recorded as Saké.

Schochu

Japanese colourless spirit obtained by distillation of the fermentation products of sweet potatoes.

Peppermint Schnapps

Dry white peppermint-flavoured pot-still spirit of the aquavit/Steinhäger/genever type which is made in Germany and U.S.A. for use in dry cocktails to replace crème de menthe.

PART II

14
The Development of Liqueurs

The production of liqueurs in past centuries was in the hands of monks in the abbeys and monasteries of Europe. The medical benefits were apparent side by side with the purely sensual pleasure of drinking them, and those early rough-and-ready mixtures frequently helped save life during the plague and disease-ridden years of our history. No doubt they were also used then as we use them now, as an enjoyable relaxant and restorative at the end of a meal. That such mixtures would have tonic powers seems obvious from the ingredients used, and although the early liqueurs were in all probability harsh to the taste, and more like medicine than the liqueurs of today, with time they were improved, maybe by ageing in wooden casks or by altering the ingredients or by changing the method of production.

The logical extension was to produce liqueurs for enjoyment only, with the medicinal benefits becoming of secondary importance. The most famous instance was the invention of a liqueur by the French doctor, Raspail, whose cure was enjoyed so much that it became commercial and world-renowned. The Goldwasser produced today is a combination of two medical superstitions, that gold was a perfect foil for diseases and caraway was the best digestive; the latter is used even now for winding babies after feeds (but called gripe water and only $4\frac{1}{2}$ per cent alcohol). Many restaurants on the Continent and America provide peppermints for diners, which is supposedly good for digestion, and recommend Crème de Menthe as a *digestif*. Very popular in Britain now are the after-dinner chocolate-mints, and the liqueur of comparable flavour, 'Royal Mint-Chocolate'.

The historical background of many liqueurs will be examined in later sections.

15
The Art of Tasting Liqueurs

It is said that the art of tasting must be inborn, and that it is impossible to become an expert without this inherited ability. No doubt there is a certain truth in this, and that those born into a family experienced in the art of tasting have a great advantage, especially of environment, which from an early age teaches the evaluation of sensual messages to the eye, the nose and the mouth. The art of tasting, however, can be learnt but it requires hard work and continuous application. It is obviously easier to study sweet liqueurs with well-defined flavours than wines with their subtleties; in the latter, the lower alcoholic strength defines small differences more strongly, which nevertheless are sometimes undetectable to the novice. The art of tasting must be practised endlessly and there are always fresh samples to examine or new products to consider. Naturally, anyone interested in serious tasting must have a sensitive palate which, with training, can become highly developed and expert.

The tasting of liqueurs can be, and usually is, a tiring and difficult job. Steady inhalation of liqueur bouquet will slowly anaesthetize the sensitive nasal buds and dull the senses. Tasting of several samples will desensitize the taste buds in the mouth and on the tongue, and generally mask minimal defects very seriously. I have found in my various experimental liqueur compoundings that a dozen closely similar samples is the maximum I can compare without my judgement being impaired. There is no doubt that for best results, six liqueur samples are maximum, twelve samples may give reasonable results which, however, require further examination and confirmation after the palate has been cleansed with water and rested for an hour.

Samples should if possible be tasted in brandy balloons, which allow the bouquet to be examined and possibly give a hint of the spirit used. Bouquet is especially important in blended products, which may use two types of spirit where harmonious co-existence is essential. The bouquet can give a taster many clues, but it is the combination of nose and palate that is essential for a balanced judgement. For the palate, a small sample should be taken which can be rolled over the tongue and the sample then rejected, if possible *in toto*. The taster should consider not only the flavour and sweetness of the liqueur, but also the 'hotness' of the spirit. The 'hotter' or sharper the spirit, the younger it is— spirits mellow with age and older spirit is much preferable to young. Essential to all good compounding is ageing in wood, which mellows and harmonizes the alcoholic and flavour ingredients; except of course for fruit spirits, which are usually aged in glass demijohns to avoid taking up colour.

The next sample should not be taken until the mouth has been rinsed with cool, clean water. In my opinion, if the taster wishes to eat between samples he should take white bread rolls and never even consider nibbling cheese. This applies equally to tasting wines. I am not a smoker, which may or may not increase my palate sensitivity; a smoker can often revive a flagging palate by a few puffs at a cigarette, but only out of doors in the fresh air. This certainly works when wines are under consideration and, by extension, should do so for liqueurs.

Basically, the only important rule is that a clean glass should be used. Nothing else really matters, although enjoyment can be immensely enhanced by serving liqueurs in very thin or finely cut glasses. The excitement for the taste buds seems to increase in direct ratio to the decreasing thickness of the glass!

Enjoyment of a liqueur follows a certain pattern:

(a) The beauty of the empty glass combined with the shape of the decanter or original bottle. This anticipates the liqueur itself and visually prepares the recipient for the enjoyment to follow.

(b) The colour of the liqueur and its flow from the bottle. At this stage, the physical response may stimulate the taste buds and give the mouth-watering effect.

(c) The nosing of the liqueur, the bouquet stimulating the nasal buds.

(d) The sipping of the liqueur, savouring the flavour on the palate.

(e) The climax on swallowing the liqueur, the warm glow in the stomach and the enjoyment of the after-taste on the palate.

Liqueurs can be enjoyed at all times of the day, with morning coffee (*eaux-de-vie* are delicious), in a cocktail for an aperitif, with coffee after lunch; aperitif cocktail before dinner, with coffee after dinner, and a liqueur to sip leisurely throughout the evening, or even as a night-time stimulant, as enjoyed by Boswell with his bedside bottles of 'strong cordials'.

In the final analysis a large glass is recommended so that the bouquet, colour and flow can be enjoyed as well as the taste, but of course, you lose more liqueur by viscous adhesion to the sides than with a small glass, as you drink.

Frequently the flavour of a liqueur will be enhanced by serving it chilled or 'on the rocks', which effectively reduces both the sweetness and alcohol, yet increases the beauty of the aroma, often illuminating high-tone bouquet nuances which are not at all apparent when the liqueur is served at room temperature.

One of the most enjoyable ways of imbibing liqueurs is in black coffee and freshly whipped cream (sugar if required). Many restaurateurs have their favourite speciality preparations. The following is a list of generally accepted names:

Speciality	*Liqueur or spirit used*
Alpine Coffee	Enzian liqueur or spirit
Belgian Coffee	Elixir d'Anvers
Calypso Coffee	Tia Maria
Caribbean Coffee	Rum
Coffee of the Glens	Glen Mist
Dutch Coffee	Genever
French (or Royal) Coffee	Cognac
Gaelic Coffee	Irish Whiskey
German Coffee	Kirsch
Italian (or Witches') Coffee	Strega
Mexican Coffee	Kahlúa
Monks' Coffee	Bénédictine; Chartreuse; Trappistine
Normandy Coffee	Calvados

Prince Charles Coffee

Royal Mint Coffee

Russian Coffee

Scandinavian Coffee

Scotch Coffee

Welsh Coffee

Westphalian Coffee

Drambuie

Royal Mint-Chocolate

Vodka

Aquavit

Scotch Whisky

Can-y-Delyn

Steinhäger

As with all drinking, you will obtain the maximum pleasure by drinking 'what you like, with whatever you like and when you like'.

16
The Classification and Labelling of Liqueurs

French liqueur manufacturers traditionally classify their products into four main groups, all of which are produced by distillation or infusion. The use of essential oils is infrequent and rather frowned upon. 'Ordinaires' include waters and oils. 'Fines' and 'Surfines' include Creams (Crèmes) and Elixirs.

Liqueur. Sweetened spirit which must contain 200 g of sugar per litre.

Demi-Fines. Standard strength is 23 per cent (20–25 kg sugar per 100 litres liqueur).

Fines. Standard strength 28 per cent (40–45 kg sugar per 100 litres liqueur).

Surfines. The finest French liqueurs are usually 30 per cent. They are the most heavily sweetened and strongest in bouquet and flavour (45–50 kg sugar per 100 litres liqueur).

'*Double*' *liqueurs* theoretically contain double quantities of flavouring materials. More usually a 50 per cent increase is used because many essential oils may produce cloudiness (by partial precipitation) in truly double concentration when the liqueur is diluted with water, as intended. The alcoholic strength and sweetness are identical with surfines.

Triple Sec. A special term which refers to curaçaos—the triple apparently has no definitive meaning as to the manufacture, although a double rectification would give a three-stage (triple) process. Curaçao Sec has the sweetness of a surfine but a strength of 44·5 per cent. Triple Sec is sweeter than Curaçao Sec, but is only

40 per cent. The full range of curaçaos (demi-fine, surfine, sec, triple sec) can be made from the same basic, dry, high-strength curaçao distillate, which is then compounded with sugar and water.

Ratafia. The name originally given to any liqueur drunk at the ratification of a treaty or agreement; surprisingly, it is derived from the Creole *tafia*, which means rum. Nowadays, it means liqueurs prepared by the infusion of fruits or nut kernels in spirits of wine. The liqueur is sweetened and additional flavouring may be added for completion.

Crème de. The term applied to liqueurs made only from the particular name type (vanille, menthe, roses, etc.); or to liqueurs such that the named flavour is predominant.

According to French law, the letters A and D must be printed on the label for sale in France, as follows:

Letter A (= aperitif) refers to wine-based aperitifs below 18° GL* (31·5° proof), aniseed-flavoured spirits below 45° GL (79° proof) (provided that they are 18° GL, less than 400 gm of sugar per litre and more than ½ gm essences per litre), and all bitters and similar products below 30° GL (52° proof).

Letter D (= *digestif*) refers to liqueurs and spirits above 15° GL (26·2° proof), with the exception of aniseeds and bitters, and wine-based aperitifs over 18° GL (31·5° proof).

Germany has special definitions:

Eis-Liköre: German liqueurs intended for drinking 'on-the-rocks'.

Kristal-Liköre: German liqueurs containing sugar crystals (cf. Italian *Mille Fiori*).

Most countries have laws that require the distiller, manufacturer or importer to specify the alcoholic content of his product on the label. It is unfortunate for the consumer that the chosen units vary from country to country—in the United Kingdom we have Proof Spirit (Sikes) (soon to be Sikes plus metric and eventually metric only) which is at variance with the American unit: in many Continental countries they state alcohol by volume percentage, in some countries by weight percentage.

* See p. 100.

Normal units

British Proof—Units known as Sikes: 100 per cent alcohol = 175° proof. System no longer in use.

Terminology: 70° proof = 30 under proof.

American Proof: 100 U.S. proof = 50 per cent alcohol by volume.

70° British proof = 80 U.S. proof.

E.E.C. alcoholic strength is given in terms of degrees Gay-Lussac (°GL), which is the percentage alcohol by volume:

Conversion to British units 40° GL=70° proof.
Conversion to U.S. units 40° GL=80° proof.

The liquid contents of liqueurs and spirits is printed on the labels as legal requisite in many countries, and most European bottle manufacturers include a figure of the total bottle capacity in the glass. This may be misleading to the consumer since this figure is the maximum liquid contents to the top lip of the bottle, and not the normal liquid content.

Britain and the U.S.A. now use metric measures (ml or cl) but the U.S.A. still uses American proof to indicate strength of her products (1 litre=100 cl=1000 ml).

160 fluid ounces per British Imperial gallon.

128 fluid ounces per American gallon.

Normal liqueur sizes

26⅔ Imperial fluid ounces	25½ U.S. fluid ounces (fifth)	75 cl
24⅔ Imperial fluid ounces	23 U.S. fluid ounces	68 cl
17 Imperial fluid ounces	16⅓ U.S. fluid ounces	50 cl
12 Imperial fluid ounces	11½ U.S. fluid ounces	34 cl

International discussions are in progress to establish standard bottle sizes for all countries. There is an obvious necessity for standardization, but it remains to be seen which sizes will be agreed if and when such changes become law. Until that time the combination of various alcoholic strength and liquid contents can be very confusing, and the Liqueurograph chart (pp. 176–7) attempts to ease this problem and also to classify liqueur types.

17

The Raw Materials for Flavouring and Making Liqueurs

Innumerable natural products from all parts of the world are suitable for preparing liqueurs and bitters. It is not practical to list all of these, but those most frequently referred to are classified according to their natural characteristics. The methods of extraction of the actual flavouring component(s) are described in the next chapter. Many of the extracted compounds have very strong flavours, and only minute quantities are used in any compounding.

Herbs

Basil, bison and other grasses, centaury, sweet clover, cocoa leaves, genip, herb ivy, hyssop, knapweed, marjoram, melissa, peppermint and other mint types, polypody, rosemary, sage, tansy, tarragon, tea leaves, bitter thistle, thyme, trefoil clover, wormwood.

Barks and Woods

Aloe, angostura, cinchona, cinnamon, guaiacum, myrrh, sandalwood, sassafras.

Drugs and Roots

Alant, angelica, blackmasterwort, calamus, celery, cloves, curcuma, galanga, gentian, ginger, henna, liquorice, lovage, orris root, rhubarb, snake root, turmeric, valerian, zedoary.

Flowers

Arnica, camomile, cinnamon, citrus blossom, clove, ivy, lavender, lily, poplar buds, rose, saffron.

Seeds and Fruits

Allspice, angelica seeds, aniseed, apricot stones, bitter almonds, cactus, cardamom, caraway (carvi and cumin), celery seeds, citrus peel, clove, cocoa, coffee, coriander, cubebs, dill, fennel, hazel nuts, juniper berries, kola nuts, mace, musk, nutmeg, peach stones, peppers (all types), pimentoes, raisins, soy beans, star anis, sweet almonds, tonka beans, vanilla.

This section also includes all edible fruits.

Miscellaneous

Honey (various types).

THE SPIRIT OF LIQUEURS

The essential ingredient, common to all liqueurs, is alcohol. This may be obtained from numerous sources in a number of ways. Important to all of these is the purity: the purer the alcohol, the finer the liqueur; by-products of alcohol production, such as fusel oils, are unwanted flavour additives. They would not necessarily be present in identical amounts in successive productions, which would yield differently flavoured end-products, and skilful compounding and manipulation would be required for corrective treatment.

Spirits used in liqueurs may be of any of the following types:

1 Neutral spirit.
2 Neutral grain spirit.
3 Whisky or whiskey.
4 Rum.
5 Grape brandy or Cognac or Armagnac.
6 Fruit spirit.
7 Rice spirit.

The quality of the spirit will depend on the following factors:

(a) The origin and the nature of the starting materials (and the fermented liquid made from them).
(b) The manner of distillation (speed, temperature, pressure).
(c) The degree of rectification.

(d) The method of maturing and alcoholic strength after distillation.

Each of the types of spirits has its special uses and often blends are made between types, e.g. whisky may be a blend of grain spirit and pot-still spirit. Unless the liqueur label specifies a particular type of spirit (whisky, Cognac, rum) the use of neutral (agricultural) or grain spirit is implied.

18

The Manufacture of Liqueurs

The flavour of liqueurs and many spirits is imparted by important groups of compounds of complicated chemical structure known as essential oils, which themselves are unpleasant and often irritating, but which in minute quantities impart ethereal and taste effects of unimaginable beauty and finesse.

Essential oils are usually liquid, but may, under certain circumstances, solidify. Each oil has its own characteristic bouquet, most are bitter to the taste, and all oxidize readily and must, therefore, be stored most carefully.

These important oils can be extracted by four methods:
(a) Pressure: oils are extracted from citrus peel under pressure in a mechanical press.
(b) Extraction with a non-volatile compound. Fats, for instance, take up the bouquets, etc., and these can later be alcohol extracted.
(c) Extraction with a volatile solvent (maceration and percolation).
(d) Distillation, which may be from aqueous solution, alcoholic solution or from a fractionation of a mixture of oils, or even a combination of these.

These oils, and other flavouring substances, are extracted from the many natural compounds used in the making of liqueurs: fruits, herbs, spices, roots, flowers, berries and leaves. The extraction of flavours is followed by compounding (which may include distillation), maturing and subsequently presentation for sale.

Selection of method of manufacture depends upon many circumstances, most of which are the personal selection of the inventor or manufacturer. Whichever method is used, best results can only be obtained by use of the finest ingredients—the spirit, the sugar and/or honey, and the flavouring materials. The delicate balance between herbs, spices, flavours, fruits, honey, etc., is the art of the liqueurist—for in obtaining this balance is the secret of success, frequently unrepeatable with similar ingredients from a different source.

Perhaps the most important decision is the balance between alcoholic strength and sweetness. The former may be strongly influenced by the spirit duty levied by governments, which has a disproportionate effect on the eventual consumer price. The latter is influenced by 'trends'—the last decade has shown definite movement towards 'dry'—a relative term, of course, but also influenced from the snob angle, it being said that those of a lower income group prefer 'sweet' products and that the higher the income group, the 'drier' the selection.

Maceration (infusion) is the extraction with cold spirit of soluble products from natural products (usually dried) until equilibrium is attained, and no further extraction takes place. The nature of the materials extracted may vary from a given mixture of raw materials, depending upon the concentration (and temperature) of alcohol in the solvent solution, and this can be specially controlled by the distiller, who may wish to extract particular products and leave others. The mixture is usually pulverized to attain maximum extraction. After maceration, the solvent is filtered gently. The filtrate, known as the aromatic infusion, may then be concentrated or even distilled. It may also be mixed with other products (compounded). The final stages of compounding and preparation for bottling are described later.

Digestion is maceration in warm solvent and usually the temperature is maintained at 40–50° C. (sometimes 60° C.) for a period of several days. Extraction is far more rapid, and more compounds are liable to be extracted than by the cold method. Sometimes the extracted products are removed by steam distillation from the mother liquors.

Percolation is a more efficient method of extraction than maceration and may be thought of as 'intensive maceration'. Pure spirit is the solvent at all times, and is passed through the natural product and therefore extracts larger quantities of soluble products than maceration. There are two practical methods possible, either continuous passage of pure spirit (cold or hot) through a column or container of the natural product, which requires large quantities of spirit, or a 'closed cycle', where a constant amount of spirit is heated to boiling point and the condensed vapours pass through the natural products, extracting the soluble components. This solution then returns into the boiling solvent and the cycle continues. This method is, of course, only suitable when the extracted compounds are stable to heat, although the solvent temperature can be lowered by using a system working at reduced pressure. The concentrated extracted products are obtained by evaporation of the spirit solvent.

Extraction by percolation is therefore more efficient than maceration, where an equilibrium position of components can be attained between solid and solution. The selection of the method of extraction is totally dependent on the nature, solubility and stability of the compounds to be extracted.

Distillation is the separation of volatile compounds from non-volatile components (tannins, colouring materials, acids, etc.), although the latter may, in small part, be carried over with volatile compounds, particularly alcohol.

Distillation may be carried out under vacuum conditions which lower the temperature of distillation and thus protect any delicate herbs, etc., which may be temperature sensitive. Either method of distillation, of course, allows definite fractions of distillate to be collected, and in many instances this 'fractionation' can be of the utmost importance—a small fraction is perfect, whereas the total distillate can be quite useless.

In any distillation process, there are three main fractions of importance.

The first is impure product of low alcoholic strength.

The second is the middle fraction, where quality and strength can be controlled by the rate of heating the still, the pressure of the system (normal atmospheric or vacuum conditions), and whether the fraction is again subdivided with a fractionating column.

The last fraction will be low-strength again, and usually useless.

The distillates, of course, are generally water-white, although some may have a very slight colour tinge. The alcoholic strength is high and the distillate is dry. It is therefore necessary to sweeten and colour the distillate to make it into an acceptable liqueur (certain fruit distillates, Kirsch, Quetsch, etc., remain dry and colourless, but are reduced in alcoholic strength with pure water). Frequently, additions are made at this stage using herb and spice extracts to add finesse, flavour and harmony to the product.

Rectification of spirits is the purification by re-distillation, which removes aldehydes, fusel oils and other impurities. Before re-distillation the spirit is reduced with water in which potash salts have been dissolved.

Preparation using extracts, ethereal oils, etc. Manufacture by mixing ethereal oils and other dissolved herb and spice extracts with the selected spirit (gin, grain spirit, brandy, whisky, etc.) is the simplest and most reproduceable method of liqueur manufacture. Some schools believe that such liqueurs are second class and that the finest liqueurs need the finesse of distillation and gentle maturing. Modern science, however, enables liqueurists to reproduce these effects without the additional expense involved, and more and more modern liqueurs use this technique.

Compounding. Most liqueurs are produced from a mixture of ingredients which themselves are obtained by the methods previously described. The compounder has exact instructions of qualities and quantities of materials and the precise method of mixing.

It is not generally realized, and I certainly did not believe it until it happened in my own experiments, that the sequence of mixing is of the utmost importance and, by changing a sequence, completely different and apparently inexplicable products can be obtained. Interaction of materials obviously causes this, but temperature differences may also give unwanted results. It must also be realized that the alcoholic solvent may affect the compounding operation and, if whisky is taken as an example, it must be remembered that no two whiskies have exactly the same acidity, and this variation of a seemingly minor point has an immense effect on the final product; a change of alcoholic solvent may necessitate a complete revision of the liqueur's formula and compounding operation.

No two compounding operations are identical, and it is the skill of the individual that brings results and continuity of flavour from these operations. In practice, it is essential to demonstrate each operation in a compounding cycle in order to achieve exactly the desired results. The final steps in any compounding operation are sweetening and maturing of the product.

Before a liqueur is ready for marketing, the various ingredients must be given time to marry together to form a single smooth product, rather than a mixture of many flavours lacking harmony and delicacy. To bring this about requires time, and the following methods are known and have been tried to shorten time:

heat	light waves
ozonization	electrolysis
movement	catalytic methods

None of the above methods has really produced acceptable results, and there appears to be no substitute for the age-old method of slow marriage and maturing in oak casks in a warehouse at a uniform cool temperature. The pores of the wooden casks allow a slight uptake of air which is necessary for 'marriage' and possibly for some of the flavour changes and transformations which are so essential for mellowing and maturing the liqueur.

Wood maturing is most important for whisky liqueurs and other liqueurs made with flavour-containing spirits where these flavours must themselves combine and mellow with the added flavours of the distiller.

The liqueur may contain colloidal materials which cannot be removed by simple filtration, and a 'fining' must often be used for clarification and precipitation of the suspension. Most commonly used are albumen, isinglass, white of egg, milk, Spanish earth, bentonite or casein.

Before bottling, the liqueur is brought to the required alcoholic strength, usually a reduction with water or sugar water, followed by colouring (if necessary) with one of the permitted colouring materials. The finished liqueur will then be bottled after filtration to remove any suspended particles, so that it is crystal-clear in its final presentation in the bottle, ready for sale.

19
Fruit Liqueurs

A certain amount of confusion exists in the British nomenclature of fruit liqueurs, which is now subject to a code of practice but no definite legal requirements.

The code may be summarized as follows: 'The description "brandy" or "fruit brandy" should only be applied to potable spirits derived from the fermented juice of fresh grapes or from the distillation of the fermented juice of other fruits.' This definition covers *eaux-de-vie*, which are discussed in Chapter 21.

The terms 'Cherry Brandy', 'Apricot Brandy' and 'Peach Brandy' are established names for sweet liqueurs made from cherries, apricots and peaches respectively, but not by the method stated above; nor are these products *eaux-de-vie*. It is agreed, however, that these two terms may be used for these liqueurs, provided that 20 per cent of the spirit content is brandy as defined above.

In the U.S.A., fruit liqueurs made by maceration of fruit in spirit and subsequent sweetening are called 'cordials'; the distilled dry spirits are called 'fruit brandies'. There is no confusion when these terms are correctly applied. Now in the United Kingdom, however, 'cordials' are flavoured drinks which can be non-alcoholic or of low alcoholic strength, although up to the mid nineteenth century, 'cordial' was used in the same sense as in the U.S.A.

Fruit liqueurs can be classified by their three methods of manufacture:

(a) Fruit juice plus spirit—a straightforward compounding operation.

(b) Maceration or percolation of the fruit with a selected

spirit followed by slight additional compounding to high-light the flavour. With stone fruits it is normal to include the kernel in the primary process. The product may be sweetened or coloured. This is the most usual manufacturing process.

(c) Distillation of the fermented mash of the fruit (with kernels) to produce the dry distilled *eau-de-vie*, fruit brandy.

GENERAL CLASSIFICATION OF FRUITS

Apples, pears.

Stone fruit: apricots, cherries, plums (different varieties), nectarines, peaches.

Berries: strawberries, raspberries, blackberries, blackcurrants and other berries.

Nuts: various edible nuts, coconut.

Citrus fruit: oranges, curaçao oranges, lemons, grapefruit, mandarins.

Tropical and other fruits: pineapples, bananas, dates, passion fruit.

CHERRY LIQUEURS

Cerasella

One of the finest Italian cherry liqueurs, supposedly the favourite of the immortal d'Annunzio. The red liqueur has a fine cherry flavour, due to the use of certain digestive herbs from the Abruzzi mountains, which give the liqueur a richness of flavour and unique quality.

Heering's Cherry Brandy

Cherry Heering is Danish and is one of the best-known and most widely distributed imported cherry brandies.

Starting from a small corner shop 160 years ago, Peter Heering established not only large sales for his special cherry brandy, but also became a shipowner of importance—an ideal combination. The company is still family owned. The shape of the bottle has returned to the traditional characteristic long-necked 'brandy' shape from the more familiar dumpy 'Bénédictine' shape.

British Cherry Brandies
These are extremely fine products. Grant's Morella Cherry Brandy has been made from brandy and Kent cherries for over a hundred years. It is lighter in texture than the imported liqueurs.

The Grants were originally a Scottish family who moved south to Sutton Valence in Kent. A descendant of these Grants was the originator of their present cherry brandy. Destruction of their Dover distillery by a cliff fall in 1853 necessitated a move in the following year to Maidstone, where their cherry brandy and other liqueurs, including cherry whisky, are produced to this day. It is of special interest that through the representation of a great-grandson of the founder, it became possible under the Finance Act 1933 for British compounders to compete 'under bond' with overseas producers.

Lamb & Watt of Liverpool produce a fine cherry brandy in the Danish style, within a range of liqueurs marketed under the brand 'Palatinate', and another excellent U.K. produced cherry brandy is 'Trotosky'—a brand also used for other liqueurs.

Cherry liqueurs are produced in many countries and by very many manufacturers. The French cherry brandies are usually light in colour and texture (Rocher, a House established at the beginning of the eighteenth century, is well known; Cherry Marnier is delicious). *Guignolet* is a term for French cherry liqueurs. The Dutch produce many fine types—one of which, de Kuyper, is the brand leader in the United Kingdom—as do, of course, the Italians and Balkan countries, whose products in the main are produced from dark cherries, giving a heavier liqueur.

Rote Kirsch
A deep-red, bitter-sweet German cherry liqueur made by Mampe.

Krambambuly
A German fiery cherry liqueur famous for generations through the student song.

Cerasella di Fra Guiepro
A Pescaran speciality made from fruit and wild cherries—bright red.

Kirsch Peureux

A sweet, water-white French cherry liqueur on a Kirsch base but quite different from Kirsch (see p. 126); it is strong and dry.

Vishnyovaya Nalivka (Russian cherry liqueur)

There are several Russian liqueurs produced by infusions of cherries, blackberries, blackcurrants and prunes.

Other Russian liqueurs are made on a similar basis to the standard West European types—a liqueur made from caraway, coriander and lemon is a sweet Kümmel type. Coffee, cherry and chocolate liqueurs are made, as are honey-sweetened liqueurs containing roots and grasses, as well as herbs and spices.

Nalivkas are sweet fruit brandies; Nastoikas are sweetened and flavoured brandies.

Wisniak and Wisniowka

Polish cherry liqueurs. The latter, which is vodka-based, is drier.

Cherry Whiskies

These have not proved as popular as cherry brandies. Chesky, made by Fremy, is French. Ross of Leith produce an excellent example better known abroad than at home. Savermo's Cherry Whiskey, formerly produced in Eire from Irish Whiskey and Czechoslovakian cherries, is no longer available. Excellent Scotch cherry whiskies have been produced at trials, but not as yet marketed, there being certain compounding difficulties in blending the acidities of cherries and Scotch whisky.

Royal Cherry-Chocolate

Pale pink French liqueur reproducing the flavour of cherry-filled chocolates. A Swiss version is Cheri-Suisse.

Maraschino

A sweet, water-white liqueur with a highly concentrated flavour. It is produced from the distillation of fermented maraschino cherries, and their crushed kernels; this variety of cherry being particularly sour, it is thought that sugar is added before fermentation; the distillate may be perfumed with Neroli or with flower-blossom extracts. Because of its intense, yet elegant flavour, maraschino is a very popular addition to many sweets—fruit salads, jellies, trifles and sorbets.

It is over two hundred years since Francesco Drioli first manufactured his Maraschino in Zara, then in the Republic of Venice. He introduced the classic Maraschino bottle, with its straw casing. Before the Second World War the three best-known firms, Drioli, Luxardo and Magazzin, manufactured in Zara in Dalmatia, centre for the amarasca, the best cherry for their liqueurs. This district is now part of Yugoslavia and, although Maraschino is still made there, Drioli is now made in Venice and Luxardo in Padua. Following the exodus of the original manufacturers in 1945, when Zara was included in the territories assigned to Yugoslavia, and the confiscation of all Italian property in the area, production was ensured by planting thousands of amarasca cherry trees, specially selected by the Tree Cultivation Institute of Florence, on the warm easterly and southerly slopes in the hills of the eastern part of the Po valley.

Many cherry liqueurs are given extra finesse and elegance by the addition of approximately 2 per cent *eau-de-vie*, usually Kirsch. This small quantity is sufficient to lift the bouquet and introduce high flavour tones which quite change the character of the liqueur, giving delicacy which can change a dull product into an excellent one.

APRICOT LIQUEURS

Every Continental, British and American liqueur producer includes an apricot liqueur in his range. The majority are made by maceration of ripe apricots with grape brandy, frequently with the addition of kernel extracts or *eau-de-vie*. Best known are the 'Abricotine' of the French firm of Garnier (whose famous distillery is at Enghien-les-Bains and who are specialists in fancy pack production and novelty bottles), Marie Brizard's 'Apry' and the Dutch Bols Apricot Brandy.

The word brandy in connection with apricot (and peach and cherry liqueurs) is, strictly speaking, a misnomer. True apricot brandy is the distilled product of fermented apricots and their kernels, a white high-strength dry *eau-de-vie*. Best-known is the Hungarian Barack Palinka. It is also made in other east European countries and by Zwack in Vienna.

Amaretto

Amarettos are beautifully balanced Italian apricot and almond liqueurs. The natural sweetness in the fruit content of the drink is subtly countered by the addition of crushed almonds. Amaretto di Saronno is well known.

The history of Amaretto is clothed in a certain mystique . . . the mystique of love. The story goes that around 1525 a poor but very beautiful widow fell in love with Bernadino Luini, who subsequently became a famous artist, and created for him a love potion, which she called Amaretto di Saronno. Bernadino, a member of the Leonardo da Vinci school, immortalized his love in a renowed fresco which to this day hangs in the Sanctuary of Santa Maria delle Grazie in Saronno.

PEACH LIQUEURS

These are made by very many manufacturers and are normally sweet and rich, produced by maceration or percolation of ripe peaches in spirit. To obtain the best flavour, extracts of the peach kernel are essential and it is not unknown for *eau-de-vie* to be added to increase the delicacy of the bouquet.

Southern Comfort

A much esteemed dry liqueur from the U.S.A., made from a base of spirit with peach flavouring, fresh peaches, oranges and herbs. It is drunk neat or in numerous mixed drinks. It has been marketed with flair and has become a best-seller in the United Kingdom. Southern Comfort is also made under licence in Eire.

BLACKBERRY LIQUEURS

(i) Sweet liqueur, prepared by the maceration of fully ripe blackberries in brandy or spirit. The product may require sweetening and *eau-de-vie* is frequently added to give finesse to the liqueur. The liqueur is made by several European producers; the Polish variety is called Jerzynowka.

A particularly fine German liqueur is made from the *Kroatzbeere*, which is similar to the blackberry. It is deep purple, not too sweet, with the wonderful bouquet of the wild blackberry.

(ii) Dry distilled blackberry brandy. See *Eaux-de-vie*, p. 128.

RASPBERRY LIQUEUR, CRÈME DE FRAMBOISES

Made by the same process as blackberry liqueurs, using fully ripe raspberries. Pagès make an interesting pink 'Framboise Sauvage' from wild raspberries grown in south-west France.

A particularly fine example with a delicious bouquet is made in Holland by Cooymans.

Rosée de France

Produced in Orleans, city of roses in the heart of the French fruit-growing region, this liqueur is made from finest raspberries grown in the Loire valley.

Royal Raspberry-Chocolate

Invented by the author, this pale red liqueur was launched in 1976, the sixth in his family of 'Royal Liqueurs'.

Chambord

French raspberry liqueur made with herbs and honey.

STRAWBERRY LIQUEUR, CRÈME DE FRAISES

Strawberry liqueur made from fully ripe strawberries by the same methods as blackberry and raspberry liqueurs.

Crème de Fraises des Bois

Liqueur made from wild strawberries cultivated to produce good yields.

BLACKCURRANT LIQUEUR, CRÈME DE CASSIS

From the sixteenth century preparations using blackcurrant leaves (and fruit) were made by monks in the Dijon area, which is ideal for growing blackcurrant bushes. The ratafia produced was offered as a universal cure for snake-bites, prevention of colds, relief of bilious attacks, and avoidance of melancholia! In 1841 Monsieur Lagoute produced a formula for 'Liqueur de Cassis' which is still marketed by his heirs today. The berries are rich in vitamin C and the liqueur is a healthy and enjoyable *digestif*.

The liqueur is made by macerating the destalked blackcurrants in grape brandy. It is sweet, red and full flavoured. A blended liqueur of blackcurrants and others is marketed by Bols as Bols-berry Liqueur.

Cassis

This is a French liqueur produced by addition of sugar to macerated blackcurrants in alcohol or *eau-de-vie*. Addition of up to 5 per cent raspberries and redcurrants is permitted; additional colouring is forbidden. In eastern Europe the liqueur was called Bocksbeeren.

FINNISH LIQUEURS

The land of the midnight sun produces wonderful liqueurs from otherwise little-known native fruits. There are three main liqueurs produced by Lignell & Piispanen and others.

Karpi

This is a fine aromatic liqueur made from cranberries (*karpalo*) and other bitter-sweet wild-growing berries from Finland's marshlands (where the fruits are also enjoyed by bears!). The fruit is often snow-covered before the end of the harvest, in which case it is picked in the spring..

Suomuurain

This is made only from cloudberries (*Rubus chamaemorus*) grown in the Arctic north. The berries are picked during the mild spring weather, and the susceptibility of the tree to sudden frost during flowering has caused the loss of many a year's crop and has thus limited the production of this very fine and delicately flavoured bitter-sweet liqueur. The liqueur is sometimes called Lakka.

Mesimarja Liqueur

Also known as the 'Red Pearl of the North'. It is a truly delight-
fully aromatic liqueur made from the Arctic Bramble (*Rubus
arcticus*).

Marli produce excellent liqueurs including arctic bramble and
ligonberry.

OTHER FRUIT LIQUEURS

Crème de Prunelle

French and Dutch liqueurs made from plums, occasionally with
the addition of a small quantity of other stone fruit including
kernels.

Prunelle Fine

Sweet Burgundy sloe liqueur obtained by sweetening *eau-de-vie*
de prunelle.

Bilberry

Blaubeere—a full-bodied liqueur produced from fermentation of
Black Forest bilberries, subsequently sweetened and coloured.

Crème de Myrtilles

A rich liqueur made by sweetening the maceration of wild bilberries in spirit. An excellent alternative to Crème de Cassis in
making an aperitif with white wine or sparkling wine.

Edel Preiselbeere

A Black Forest cranberry speciality liqueur. For plum brandies,
see *Eaux-de-vie*, p. 127.

Sir Frederick's Wild Strawberry

Wild strawberries macerated in old brandy to a seventeenth-
century formula.

Crème d'Ananas, Pineapple Liqueur

An excellent golden pineapple liqueur on a rum base is made by Lamb & Watt, and obtains its special flavour by long maturing in wooden casks. A Hawaiian type is available in the U.S.A., and a Dutch variety, Tornado, is made by Hulstkamp from an old recipe based on Hawaiian fruit.

Crème de Banane, Banana Liqueur

A sweet yellow liqueur made by maceration of ripe bananas in pure spirit. The liqueur usually has a very strong banana bouquet and is made in many countries, including Australia. Mus is a Turkish brand.

Royal Banana-Chocolate

A French blend of banana and chocolate.

Nezhinskaya Ryafina

Sweet Russian rowan-flavoured brandies with a sharp taste.

Rabinowka

Another form of rowanberry liqueur from East European countries; imported pre-war from Riga.

Sabra

A mild, red bitter-sweet liqueur originally made in Israel from the hardy desert sabra cactus. This fruit grows in the Mediterranean region of Africa, and is found in rocky desert land. Presentation is still in a reproduction of a Phoenician jug although the liqueur is now orange- and chocolate-flavoured.

Zolotaya Osen (Golden Autumn)

Caucasian damson, apple and quince liqueur; bitter-sweet.

Verana

A Spanish fruit liqueur from Seville.

There are many German liqueurs such as 'Kirsch mit Whisky', 'Aprikose mit Whisky', etc., which are fruit liqueurs based on spirit and whisky; the latter may be local whisky or partly imported whisky. If the whisky origin is not stated in any form it may be assumed to be local produce.

Sloe Gin

The traditional 'stirrup cup' of Old England. It is a rich, deep-red liqueur made by steeping ripe unblemished sloe berries (the fruit of the blackthorn bush) in gin. Other fruits may occasionally be added to increase the flavour, depending upon the quality of the crop. The liqueur is matured in wood, and the finished liqueur has valuable astringent properties, good for the digestion.

Pedlar brand made by Hawkers of Plymouth, who have supplied the Royal Household for three hundred years, is best known of the British sloe gins—their 'gold label' is *de luxe* quality made from hand-picked sloes in the best years; others are produced by Ross of Leith, Lamb & Watt, and Nicholsons.

20

Citrus Liqueurs

~~~~~~~~~~~~~~~~~~

CURAÇAO

The original orange curaçao was made with fruit from the Island of Curaçao, but the term has become generic and is also used for liqueurs made from oranges of other origins.

The flesh of the orange is discarded, only the peel being used, and it is most important that the oranges be gathered at the correct time. The fine flavours are extracted by soaking in water, then steeping in spirit, followed by distillation and rectification. Many Dutch distillers import dried orange peel from Curaçao, which retains the essential oils and other flavour compounds.

Excellent Curaçaos are made by Bols and Fockink in Holland and by most French producers, and they are available in many colours—orange, brown, white, blue and green. Visitors to Amsterdam should not miss a visit to Wynand Fockink's Tasting Room with its unique atmosphere and delightful drinking ceremony, where a range of Curaçaos and other liqueurs can be enjoyed. Triple-sec White Curaçao is water-white, highly rectified curaçao; see p. 98.

Cointreau

The most popular of the triple-sec Curaçaos. Because of imitations of the bottle and the label before the war, the brand name 'Cointreau' replaced the old title 'Triple-sec', which was, and still is, used by other distillers.

Towards the middle of the 1800s, Edouard Cointreau's son, Edouard *fils*, was given the assignment of representing the firm, who were confectioners and liqueurists in Angers, abroad. One of his sales routes took him to the West Indies and there he discovered the orange, which grows so prolifically in a warm climate. At that time oranges were not at all common in Europe, though Confucius tells us that five hundred years before Christ the Chinese were cultivating sweet oranges in the provinces of Chekiang and Kwangtung. In Europe only bitter oranges were known before the fifteenth century, and these reached Spain only in the ninth century, in the wake of Arab conquest. Four more centuries passed before the bitter was joined by the sweet, and until the end of the nineteenth century oranges were a relatively rare and much prized delicacy.

Arab ships brought oranges from the Ganges valley to Red Sea ports. The fruit was taken from there by camel train to ports in Palestine before setting forth on the last stage of their journey to islands in the Mediterranean.

The orange discovered by Edouard *fils* was a species of wild orange native to the islands of the Caribbean. Knowing the perishable fruit could not survive the long ocean voyage back to France, the enterprising scion of the Cointreau family had a quantity of the small tropical oranges peeled and the peel dried. Then he sent the aromatic peel home to Angers. The unusual scent of the peels stirred the imagination of Edouard Cointreau *père*, and he began experimenting. Tirelessly he sought the best method for bringing out the delicate scent and flavour. He steeped the peel in the finest brandies and through distillation combined the infusions with various regional herbs and spices.

The flavour from the peel of any fruit is naturally different from the flavour of the fruit itself. The peel contributes a tartness, or even bitterness, which accounts for the slight 'bite' that distinguishes liqueurs made from peels from the fruit liqueurs. The work with the bitter peel from the Caribbean led to experimentation in blending that peel with the peel of other varieties of sweet oranges. Eventually, an outstanding balance of flavours and aromas was produced. It was not until the 1870s and the advent of railways and the first international exhibitions that the fame of the drink spread outside France. The formulation has a special kind of taste, which has made it very popular the world over.

Grand Marnier

One of the best-known Curaçaos, which is made at Neauphle-le-Château and at Château-de-Bourg. The manufacturing company, Ets. Marnier Lapostolle, was founded in 1827 and from modest beginnings the company grew until, in 1880, Grand Marnier was invented, based on Cognac and distinguished by the fact that the spirit base is exclusively Cognac. The subtle bouquet is produced by distillation of the orange steeped in Cognac, and the excellent blending of the liqueur produces a superb, inimitable masterpiece. Two qualities are marketed—Cordon Rouge and Cordon Jaune, the latter of lower strength.

Aurum

A golden fruit and herb liqueur based on the orange, but 'spiked with the pungent peel', produced at Pescara, Italy. The spirit is old brandy, and all the ingredients are harvested in the Abruzzi mountains.

Old Jamaica Wild Orange Liqueur

A delicious orange and rum liqueur made to the Sangster family formula.

Fes

A German high-quality liqueur made from pure orange juice.

Ben Shalom (Son of Peace)

An Israeli liqueur, rich and mellow, produced from Jaffa oranges.

Pomeranzen Liqueurs

Mainly German liqueurs of the Curaçao type based on unripe Pomeranzen oranges; green and orange, sometimes called gold.

Halb und Halb, Half-om-Half

German and Dutch liqueurs, usually an equal blend of orange Curaçao and orange bitters.

Mersin

Turkish triple-sec Curaçao, named after the port on the south coast of Turkey.

Royal Orange-Chocolate

Invented by the author in 1969, the smooth combination of orange and chocolate has proved to be a very popular item in the 'Royal Liqueur' range.

Utu

A new Danish orange-based liqueur produced by Heering recalling the romantic legend of Utu, the Sun God.

Van der Hum

This is a South African liqueur made from an orange-type fruit—the *naartjies*—and flavoured with other fruits, plants, seeds and barks. While there is no exact record of the origins, it is obvious that the Dutch settlers made this liqueur in imitation of their well-loved Curaçao. The name Van der Hum arose from settlers being unable to remember the name of the inventor, and is in translation 'Mr What's-his-name'. Bertrams has been made for a century, and is the best known, but there are many fine Van der Hums produced.

Crème de Mandarine (Tangerine)

Liqueurs obtained from the dried peel of the tangerine, similar to the production of Curaçao from oranges. Dutch and French varieties are excellent, from various producers; the Danish 'San Michele' is particularly well known.

Mandarine Napoléon

Manufactured by the internationally renowned Belgian company Fourcroy, this liqueur is made by macerating mandarin peel in selected old brandies. After maceration and distillation the spirit is compounded with the flavour and sweetened to produce a lightly flavoured unique product. It is said to be made from the recipe with which Napoleon wooed his favourite actress, Mlle Mars.

Forbidden Fruit

This is an old American liqueur originally with a fine citrus flavour and bitter-sweet tang originating from the shaddock (which is an unusual fruit of the grapefruit family), blended seductively with honey and orange. Recently the flavour has been changed to apple. The liqueur was served and popularized by Del Monico in New York. It has been said that this liqueur was so good that it was 'Nectar of the Gods—forbidden to man'. The liqueur is marketed in a uniquely attractive orb-shaped bottle decorated with gilt filigree.

Lemon Liqueur

This is a typical citrus liqueur. The citron variety is rich in essential oils, which give flavours to the liqueur; also added are extracts of flower petals and oil of Neroli. The citron of Mampe-Berlin is delicious. Some lemon liqueurs are marketed as Bergamot Liqueur, the name of a special lemon variety grown in Mediterranean countries to produce bergamot oil for the perfumery industry. The Austrian variety is confusingly called Kaiserbirnlikor.

Royal Lemon-Chocolate Liqueur

First marketed in 1977, it was introduced to celebrate Queen Elizabeth's Silver Jubilee.

Royal Tangerine-Chocolate Liqueur

A fairly recent, delicate combination of chocolate and tangerine (mandarin) flavours.

O'Jaffa

An Israeli liqueur produced from maceration of mixed citrus fruits and distillation. The flavour has a hint of grapefruit, the delicate bouquet of tangerine and full flavour of the Jaffa orange.

Citronen-eis Likor

A yellow German liqueur made from lemon juice and lemon peel distillate, intended for drinking 'on-the-rocks'.

Kitron

Greek spirit obtained by distillation of grape brandy with leaves of lemon trees. The product may be sweetened into a liqueur.

Cayo Verde

An American liqueur, light in texture, made from key limes and spirit.

Filfar

A Curaçao-type liqueur made in Cyprus from a fermented mixture of citrus fruit and herbs. The recipe, which is said to originate from the monks of Cantara Monastery near Famagusta, is now owned by Mr Takis Philippou.

Parfait Amour

An exotic, sweet citrus-oil based liqueur. It is scented and slightly spiced and is very similar to Crème de Violettes, with additional flavour from flower petals. It is made in several colours, mainly bright violet, by most major European producers.

Passion Fruit Liqueur

A deep golden, sweet citrus-flavoured liqueur made in Australia. A brand is Grand Cumberland.

Bantu

A German liqueur based on tropical passion fruit.

Capricornia

This is another Australian liqueur made from tropical fruits.

Pimpeltjens

One of Holland's oldest liqueurs, this de Kuyper Nassau orange speciality has been made for more than three centuries and is presented in a Delft design bottle.

Poncio

An Italian citrus and vanilla liqueur from Molise.

Paradiso

A Dutch grapefruit liqueur.

Quartet

A multi-citrus liqueur (orange, tangerine, lemon and lime), specially composed for the London Philharmonic Orchestra's Golden Anniversary (1982).

Rock and Rye

American liqueurs made by steeping citrus and other fruits in rye whiskey. The name is derived from the original liqueur, which was rock candy crystallized on the sides of the bottle and rye whiskey.

Hallelujah

A new Israeli orange liqueur.

21

Fruit Brandies

Eaux-de-Vie ('Waters of Life')

These are dry fruit brandies usually bottled at higher alcoholic strength (approximately 45° GL = 79° proof) than liqueurs and infrequently aged before bottling.

The finest 'classic' fruit brandies come from Alsace, the Black Forest area of Germany and the German-speaking part of Switzerland. The French products are usually bottled in white flute bottles, the German and Swiss products in highly decorative squat bottles.

These colourless strong brandies are clean and strong and at their best when served lightly chilled at the end of a meal, although in Germany and Switzerland they are enjoyed as a Schnapps with morning coffee.

Eaux-de-Vie-de-Cidre (de-Poire)

Fruit spirit obtained by distillation of cider (apple wine) or perry (pear wine).

Poire Williams

The *eau-de-vie* produced by distilling the fermented juice of the Williams pear. This brandy is often sold in a pear-shaped bottle containing a ripe pear, which was grown in the bottle as it hung on the tree.

The Swiss producers frequently age pear brandy in wooden casks, after which it is bottled at high strength.

Produced in Switzerland, Alsace, Provence and Germany.

Liqueur Poire William

The best sweetened *eaux-de-vie*, such as Manguin of Avignon, have the elegant bouquet of the pear with a lightly balanced sweetness emphasizing the subtle flavour of the ripe pears.

Kakshe

High-strength Nepalese spirit obtained by distillation of fermented local fruits.

Kirsch, Quetsch and other Stone-fruit Brandies

It is essential to include crushed kernels in the fruit juice, which is fermented and twice distilled in pot-stills, as they give a fine bitter tang to the brandy. The water-white brandies cannot be aged in wood, since this would give them colour. The fragrance of the fruit brandies is preserved by bottling soon after distillation at fairly high strength or by storage in large glass containers.

Eau-de-vie de Kirsch = cherry; *prune* = plum; *quetsch* = Switzen plum; *Mirabelle* = Mirabelle plum.

Kirschwasser

This is the German Black Forest speciality, whose special quality is attributed to the site, the soil and the selection of the cherry type. The name *-wasser* (water) is surely a misnomer for high-strength dry-flavoured spirit!

One matter should be stressed: it is of the utmost importance in the manufacture of a fine product that the distillation should be rapid after the end of the fermentation of the fruit mash, for all fruit wines are readily spoiled by acetobacter (bacteria which turn alcohol to vinegar). Fruit brandies, Kirsch in particular, are frequently added to sweet fruit liqueurs to add finesse, elegance and bouquet.

Plum Brandies

Mirabelle and Switzen plums are the basis of excellent flavoursome brandies, produced on the same principle as Kirsch, called Mirabelle and Quetsch (Zwetschenwasser or Zwetgenwasser) respectively. Both are water-white, bottled at high strength, and produced in France, Germany, Switzerland and in many Balkan countries, where they are collectively called *slivovitz* (*slivovica* in Yugoslavia, *slibovitz* in Romania). The latter uniquely may be cask-matured when, naturally, some colour may be taken up.

Serbian plum and juniper brandy is called *klekovaca*; Romanian plum brandy with almond flavour is *tzuica*.

The *eaux-de-vie* from Alsace are world-renowned for their delicate flavour and are strongly alcoholic in taste. The majority of popular flavours, produced in quantity, are made by distillation of the fermented fruit, but many are prepared by maceration in neutral *eau-de-vie* for several weeks to extract the delicate flavour, which would be destroyed by the heat of the distillation process.

Distilled eaux-de-vie	*Macerated production*
Quetsch	*Framboise (raspberry)
Kirsch	Fraises (strawberry)
Mirabelle	Mûre (mulberry)
Cassis	Sureau (elderberry)
Apricot	Sorbier (rowanberry)
*Poire Williams	Gratte-Cul (hollyberry)
Prunelle (sloe)	Baix de Houx (hips)
Vogelbeer (berries of mountain ash or rowan)	

Other spirits are Gentiane (gentian), Coing (quince), Myrtille (bilberry), Reine Claude (greengage), Eglantine (rose hips), Alisier (sorb apple).

The *eaux-de-vie* are always bottled at high strength and those marked * are also occasionally made into sweet liqueurs. Production is very much on a small scale, with the individual producers taking great pride in the high quality of their manufacture.

Apricot Brandy

See pp. 109, 113.

Soft Fruit Brandies (*Eaux-de-Vie*)

Very fine, delicately flavoured brandies are produced from soft fruit—raspberries, strawberries, blackberries, etc. With all fruit brandies it is absolutely essential to control the fermentation temperature; low temperature slows the fermentation, too high a temperature will lose bouquet and flavour. The range 20°–22° C. is considered best.

Eau-de-vie de

Framboise (raspberry)—France, Germany, Switzerland (Himbeergeist).

Fraise (strawberry)—France, Germany, Switzerland (Erdbeergeist).

Fraises de Bois (wild strawberry)—France, Germany, Switzerland.

Blackberry—France (Mûre), Germany, Switzerland (Brombeergeist).

Fig—Morocco and other Mediterranean countries.

German nomenclature differentiates between fruit brandies termed *-wasser* and *-geist*. 'Wasser' (e.g. Kirschwasser) are produced by distillations of the fermented fruit mash. 'Geist' (e.g. Himbeergeist) are produced by maceration of the fruit in alcohol followed by distillation. This method is essential for soft fruits with a low sugar content.

German apple and pear brandies are classified as 'Branntwein'.

22

Herb Liqueurs

Drambuie

The oldest and most famous whisky liqueur, Drambuie is based on a private recipe originating from Prince Charles Edward Stuart, Bonnie Prince Charlie. Legend has it that after the unsuccessful eighteenth-century rebellion, the '45, when the Scottish rebels were completely defeated at the battle of Culloden Moor, it was one of the hunted prince's Highland friends, Mackinnon of Strathaird, who gave him shelter and successfully found him transport to France. As a mark of personal gratitude and affection, the Prince is said to have presented his personal recipe to Mackinnon, whose family to this day produce and market it as Drambuie —the Gaelic for the 'drink that satisfies'. Rich in flavour, Drambuie uses fine mature malt whiskies as its base.

Glen Mist, Scotch Whisky Liqueur

In terms of ancient recipes, Glen Mist is young (pre-war), but nevertheless, it is the second oldest of all whisky liqueurs, invented by Hector MacDonald. It is now produced again, to a modern formula, by the author in Scotland after its eighteen-year excursion to Eire. At the beginning of the Second World War the recipe was purchased by Savermo Ltd, who appointed S. F. & O. Hallgarten as sole distributors for their Glen Mist. When Scotch whisky supplies became impossible, and honey and sugar unobtainable in austerity Britain of 1945, production was taken to Eire by S. F. Hallgarten, until it returned to Scotland in 1963. While it was made in Eire the base was Irish whiskey. During this period world-wide export and British supplies were directed from Eire, and in order to avoid marketing misunderstanding another liqueur was created parallel to Glen Mist production—Irish Mist.

A third, much drier liqueur, 'Whisqueur', was produced during the period when Scotch whisky was in short supply.

Glen Mist is a blend of flavours, honey and only the highest-quality fully-matured Scotch whisky used as its base. The liqueur is matured in whisky casks for several months and is totally produced and bottled in Scotland. Of the several Scotch liqueurs internationally marketed, Glen Mist is the driest and is, therefore, much appreciated by connoisseurs of good food and drink.

In the U.S.A., where the term 'Scotch Whisky Liqueur' means a half-bottle of Scotch whisky (slightly sweetened with sugar), Glen Mist is marketed as 'Scotland's Finest Liqueur'.

Glayva

A herb and spice liqueur, produced after the war by Ronald Morrison in Scotland.

Clanrana

A modern liqueur made in Scotland.

Lochan Ora

A modern Scotch whisky liqueur, flavoured with honey.

Redalevn

A dry Scotch whisky liqueur unique to Manchester United Football Club, named after their famous team, the 'Red Eleven'.

Can-y-Delyn

A recent liqueur inspired by the mountains and valleys of Wales. Based on whisky and honey, Can-y-Delyn is considered to be a dryish liqueur.

Lindisfarne Liqueur

An English liqueur made on a whisky base with honey.

Irish Mist

A herb and honey liqueur based on Irish whiskey. Developed by the liqueur company originally created in Eire together with Irish interests by Savermo Ltd, and its managing director, S. F. (Fritz) Hallgarten, during the time when Glen Mist production was transferred to Tullamore.

Bénédictine

About the year 1510 the learned monk Don Bernardo Vincelli, at Fécamp, is said to have discovered this great elixir which, when consumed in modest quantities, revived the tired monks.

The elixir was used to combat malarial diseases prevalent in the countryside around the monastery, no doubt a most popular medicine with fishermen and peasants alike. In 1534 Francis I, King of France, visited the monastery and praised the elixir, which was known as 'Benedictine ad majorem Dei gloriam'—'Benedictine for the greater glory of God'. The Fécamp Abbey was destroyed during the French Revolution and the Order dispersed. The recipe, however, was entrusted to the Procureur Fiscal of the Abbey and later came into the hands of Monsieur Alexandre le Grand, a wine merchant and descendant of the original trustee.

The recipe was successfully used to reconstruct the original liqueur and Bénédictine is now shipped to many countries, each bottle bearing the title D.O.M.—'Deo Optimo Maximo'—'To God, most good, most great'.

It interested me to hear that large quantities are shipped to Malaysia, where it is very popular with Chinese workers in the tin mines, who spend hours knee-deep in water at their work. Tradition has it that Bénédictine helps to prevent rheumatism and other muscular aches.

B. & B.

Bénédictine and Brandy is a drier version of Bénédictine and more to the current popular taste, particularly in North America.

Chartreuse

The Carthusian Order was founded by St Bruno almost nine hundred years ago, at Chartreuse, near Grenoble in the French Alps. Over the centuries the monastery was rebuilt several times, usually following destruction by fire, and the present building at Voiron is almost three hundred years old. The production of the liqueur was unknown outside the monastery until 1848, when a group of army officers quartered there were offered a liqueur as *digestif* after dinner. Needless to say, it was found to be extraordinarily fine and they promised to spread word of the discovery. Demand increased rapidly, so that by 1860 it was necessary to build a distillery at Fourvoirie to cope with it. In 1903 the Carthusians were expelled from France, and continued to make their liqueur in Tarragona, where they found refuge, until their return to France in 1931. During exile they advertised 'Demandez une Tarragone' and pointed out that the liqueur was the same, only the bottle being different.

Several years ago I tasted a bottle of Chartreuse which was approximately a hundred years old. The dark green bottle was etched with the name, but without indication of strength. The liqueur was pale yellow, not dissimilar to today's product, surprisingly enough with less herbal flavour and spicier alcohol tones—a delicious tasting experience.

Chartreuse is marketed at two strengths: 55 per cent (green) and 43 per cent (yellow). Imitations abound, but although many are of similar type and character, none can equal the flavour and finesse of the original recipe of the Carthusian monks. There was a time, however, when a licence was granted to manufacture Chartreuse; unfortunately, there are no records available about this arrangement, neither the quantity produced, nor the distribution achieved.

Other Chartreuse liqueurs are:

V.E.P. (vieillissement exceptionellement prolongée)

At least twelve years' maturing in wood.

Elixir Végétal Chartreuse

The oldest of the liqueurs (1737) with restorative properties; used medicinally. Sold in small bottles at very high strength (71 per cent).

Orange and Myrtille

Two fruit-flavoured liqueurs.

There are many French, and other, Chartreuse imitations, *liqueurs jaunes* and *liqueurs vertes*. Many of the French ones are localized and I recall tasting an excellent brand, Grignan (45 per cent) in the Rhône-Ventoux region, which is made by Trappist monks. German imitations are generically named 'Kartäuser'; imitations of Bénédictine are called Diktiner. Monastique is a similar liqueur.

Cordial Médoc

This is a flavoury sweet red liqueur based on old claret flavoured with herb extracts. It is produced in Bordeaux.

Izarra (Basque for 'Star')

Izarra is produced in two forms—green (48 per cent) and yellow (35 per cent). It has been made since 1835 from an old recipe. Production is on an Armagnac base with flavouring drawn from plants grown in the French Pyrenees.

Trappistine

A very old formula in the possession of the monks of the Abbey of Grâce-Dieu, in France, is still used to produce Trappistine. The liqueur, which is pale green-yellow, is produced from freshly gathered herbs from the Doubs mountains and is based on Armagnac. It is sold in characteristically shaped bottles at 43 per cent.

La Vieille Cure

This liqueur has been produced at the Abbey of Cenon in the Gironde district since mediaeval times. It is made from a secret formula, and its preparation entails maceration of fifty root and aromatic plants in Armagnac and Cognac.

Fior d'Alpi (Flower of the Alps)

There are several fine Italian herb liqueurs; one of the best— Mille Fiori, which is assumed to contain extracts from a thousand flowers—was made by Distilleria Vigevanese. Others are called Isolabella and Edelweiss.

The liqueurs are presented in tall white flute bottles containing a 'Christmas tree' made of a small twig on which hang crystals of sugar. The liqueurs are smooth and reviving. Certain difficulties are experienced with importation, as the actual contents of bottles varies, as does the alcoholic strength, owing to the liqueur being bottled when warm and containing large amounts of sugar which crystallize on the twig as the liqueur slowly cools.

Galliano

Galliano liqueur is a pale amber colour and is made from high-quality spirit blended with herbs, roots and flowers. It is available in a unique and elegant, long-tapered bottle.

The liqueur was named after a Major Giuseppe Galliano, a member of the Italian Expeditionary Corps in the Italian-Abyssinian conflict of 1895–6, as a tribute to his heroic stand at the fort of Enda Jesus, where he held out for forty-four days before being ordered to surrender. The Italian poet Pascoli, in his ode to Galliano, has written, 'Preserve your wine, for one day soon, wrapped in his flag, Galliano returns.' Pictured on the label of the Galliano liqueur bottle is, in fact, the fort of Enda Jesus.

Liqueur Galliano is made at Salara, fifteen miles north of Milan, in one of Europe's most highly mechanized and modern distilleries. The liqueur is stored for up to six months in glass tanks to allow a proper marriage of the ingredients before being repeatedly filtered and then bottled.

The drink has become well known internationally through a very fortunate incident concerning one Harvey—a surfer who liked to ride the big Californian waves. After losing one important contest, Harvey consoled himself with his favourite drink, a Screwdriver (orange juice and vodka) with a splash of Galliano liqueur; apparently he imbibed a little more than usual and was seen by his friends literally to bounce from wall to wall as he left the bar. The event earned Harvey the nickname of 'the wall-banger', and hence the Harvey Wallbanger.

Strega

According to legend, beautiful maidens disguised as witches once mixed a magic drink in the city of Benevento. Tradition decrees that when two people taste this drink they are for ever united. Strega is a neutral yellow Italian liqueur made from the flavours of over seventy herbs and barks, to a formula which may be centuries old. It is a popular liqueur drunk neat and is very good (as are all fine liqueurs) with ice-cream.

Tuaca

Legend has it that this Italian demi-sec liqueur of indescribable taste was secretly formulated for Lorenzo the Magnificent, the powerful ruler of majestic Florence, renowned for the grandeur of his hospitality.

Elixir d'Anvers

A full-flavoured, soft but not too sweet after-dinner liqueur made by de Beukelaer in Antwerp. The herbs and seeds used in the production of this green-yellow liqueur give a fine bitter-sweet flavour. It is still made by the old-fashioned methods to ensure continuity, and is recognized as the Belgian national liqueur.

Elixir de Spa

The town of Spa has been famous as a watering place from the twelfth century, and in the Middle Ages many royal persons visited it to take the cure.

In 1643 Capuchin Friars took up residence near Spa under the patronage of Walter de Livorlo, and these friars invented an elixir made from distilled extracts of local plants. A sweet liqueur, the elixir was recommended for its tonic and digestive qualities. The monastery was dissolved in 1797. The formula was, fortunately, found in a manuscript from the old library, and it is still being used for regular production.

Calisay

A Spanish liqueur of sweetened spirit flavoured with cinchona and other barks.

Cuaranta-y-Tres

Spanish herb liqueur made, as its name suggests, from forty-three herbs. It is golden in colour.

Sapindor

Liqueur de Sapin is made from plants grown in the Jura mountains. The base is spirit and it has been produced in Pontarlier since 1825. The bottle is shaped and coloured like the bark of a tree—the liqueur is green, pleasantly aromatic with a spicy taste.

Brontë

A Yorkshire liqueur based on brandy with honey and herb flavouring. Distributed in a characteristic pottery container.

Angelica Liqueur

A sweet Basque liqueur flavoured with angelica and Pyrenean plants. There is an East German variety, which includes violet extracts.

Aiguebelle

Aiguebelle liqueur comes from a Trappist Abbey set in some remote hills ten miles from Montélimar.

In 1137 the Abbey of Notre Dame d'Aiguebelle was founded by the monks of an expanding Trappist Order. The rigid Trappist philosophy demands industry and dedication, and through the Middle Ages and beyond the monks were able to live only the most primitive rural existence. The Abbey was abandoned at the time of the French Revolution, but shortly afterwards, in 1815, enterprising Swiss Trappists arrived to restart the community.

Aiguebelle liqueur was first made at the turn of the nineteenth century in green and yellow forms. Père Hughes discovered the recipe when he found an ancient parchment with 'Formule de la liqueur Frère Jean'.

The liqueur is made by macerating several dozen Provençal plants, roots and herbs in alcohol, followed by slow distillation, maturing and sweetening. It is spicy and supposedly has marvellous restorative properties. The green liqueur is drier than the yellow.

Carlsberg

A bitter Czechoslovakian liqueur made from selected herbs and selected thermal waters. It also has been made in West Germany since the war.

Carmeline

Carmeline was produced in Bordeaux until several years ago. It was a neutral, green-yellow herb liqueur.

China-China

A French liqueur made from spices and other flavours.

Cocuy
A Venezuelan brandy distilled from fermented sisal roots.

Elixir Amorique
Green herb liqueur from Brittany.

Enzian Liqueurs
Bavarian liqueurs made from mountain gentian plants. A distilled, strongly scented brandy is also made in alpine parts of Germany, France and Switzerland. It is valued medicinally for stomach pains.

Ettaler
German herb liqueurs available yellow (42 per cent) and green (44 per cent). They are made in Kloster Ettel, a Benedictine monastery near Oberammergau.

Gorny Doubnyak
A Russian bitter liqueur made from an infusion containing oils of ginger, galingale, angelica root, clove, acorns and oak shavings.

Ginger Liqueurs
Made by maceration of ginger root in pure spirit. A very fine Dutch ginger liqueur is marketed by Berry Bros. & Rudd Ltd, of London, known as 'The King's Ginger Liqueur'. It is golden, dryish, with a pronounced spicy ginger bouquet and crisp flavour, and is said to have been a favourite liqueur of King Edward VII.

Royal Ginger-Chocolate
One of the author's modern liqueurs, a subtle blend of fine ginger and chocolate. Made and bottled in France.

Jägermeister
A dark red German herb liqueur.

Liqueur des Moines
'Liqueur of the Monks'—an excellent yellow digestive produced from aromatic plants and old matured Cognac.

Monte Aguila

A Jamaican liqueur introduced after the war which is not available generally in the United Kingdom. The liqueur is made from Jamaican ingredients, the dominant flavour is pimento (allspice). The liqueur is slightly bitter and an excellent digestive.

Raspail

A yellow French liqueur, based on herbs, originated by François Raspail in 1847. Raspail is proclaimed as the forerunner of Pasteur; the former believed that his liqueur would possess digestive and medicinal properties. Although he was not qualified, he was very interested in medical problems, and originally named his liqueur 'Veritable liqueur hygiénique et de dessert'. The recipe contains angelica, calamus, myrrh and other interesting natural products. It is still produced at Cenon by a subsidiary of Bols.

La Senancole

A yellow herb liqueur, aromatic and spicy, originally made by the monks of the Abbey de Senanque, founded by the Cistercian Order in 1148, at Salon, Provence. According to local tradition, Saint Bernard himself chose the site of the monastery.

It is recorded that one of the priors, Dom Marie Augustin, used local plants, which grew in abundance, and invented a delicately flavoured *digestif* which he named 'La Senancole' after the river torrent which flows at the foot of the valley below the Abbey. The liqueur has been privately made since 1930, under the supervision of the prior, from the herbs which are still gathered by the monks. It is still to be found in France, particularly in and around Marseilles.

Sève

A sweetened orange-coloured and flavoured herb liqueur made by Fournier-Demars, at St Amand (Cher). Other producers also manufacture Sève liqueurs based on Cognac or Fine Champagne.

St Hallvard

An interesting golden-coloured Norwegian liqueur. It is made from neutral potato spirit subtly flavoured with herbs and aromatic botanicals.

Stonsdorfer

A dark German bitter herb liqueur.

Tapio

A herb and juniper liqueur based on an old Finnish recipe. It is water-white with a good, dry herbal flavour.

Verveine du Velay

Two original liqueurs are made by Pagès, in south-west France, green and yellow; both are herb liqueurs with a sharp bitter flavour.

Himalayan Peak

An Indian liqueur not yet distributed in Europe.

Angelique

A greenish liqueur with very spirity flavour.

Suc de Monbazillac

In 1512 the Cardinal Albret visited Bergerac and asked the Governor's wife if the ladies of the region enjoyed this 'suc'. 'No,' she is said to have replied, 'but they would give plenty to their husbands to make their passion more ardent and their love more profound.' It is made in the Dordogne and offered as green and yellow types.

Royal Colombier

A golden-yellow liqueur made from two dozen herbs in Saumur.

Pedrocchino

A golden-green, very herby 'monkish' liqueur invented in 1904 and now made in Padua.

Zafaran

An Indian classical-style liqueur made from herbs and Himalayan botanicals with the Zafaran herb flavour predominating.

Alpestre

An Alpine herbal liqueur produced by the Maristi fathers of Carmagnola.

Anthemis

A pale green herbal mint liqueur produced by the Benedictine monks at Montevergine.

Strahl 90

A high-strength German herb liqueur, known in Germany as Flensburger Leuchtfeuer, the lighthouse where during his lonely watch the keeper invented this recipe.

Chicuva

A Spanish liqueur made from very old sherry, brandy and a secret recipe of herbs.

Wild Turkey

A successful Bourbon liqueur made in the U.S.A.

23

Liqueurs with One Herb Flavour Predominating

Absinthe

A product now banned, in its original form, in many countries. Historically, absinthe was a very dry and bitter spirit of high alcoholic strength made from many aromatic herbs, including aniseed, liquorice, fennel, hyssop, coriander, orris root and wormwood, all of which are grown in the Jura mountains. It was marketed by Henri Louis Pernod, who built a large trade for it until it was banned by France and Switzerland just before the First World War. Imitation absinthes are marketed in which the dangerous ingredient, wormwood, is replaced by other components, such as aniseed.

The most widely distributed absinthe substitute is Pernod Anis, which, although available at a lower strength than the original, appears to be a similar elixir, and is consumed in identical fashion —dry with water and ice, which turns it milky. In Edwardian days many women found absinthe too dry and remedied this by pouring the liqueur dropwise through a lump of sugar perched on a special absinthe spoon.

Aniseed-flavoured drinks have various origins. In the south of France, for instance, the flavour is obtained from fennel (green aniseed); it can also be taken from aniseed originating in the east but grown in Spain. But the aniseed found in Pernod, which gives it its distinctive taste, nearly all comes from the 'badiane', or Chinese aniseed tree. This large tree, which is of the magnolia family, is grown in North Vietnam and, after many unsuccessful tests, it seems that it cannot be grown in any other part of the world.

Its fruit is known as 'star aniseed' (*anis étoile*), and is shaped like a star with seven or eight arms, the peel of which is quite tough. Inside each of these 'arms' is an oval mahogany-red grain which contains a strong aromatic agent. These grains can be used directly as raw materials, but, because of the volume needed by the producers and the complications arising for their transport to Europe, the distillers have found it easier and more logical to distil it on the spot to extract the more easily transportable oil. When it arrives in France, this natural oil is purified by re-distillation.

Aniseed drinks are extremely popular in France, the market being shared between Pernod and Pastis drinks. The main difference is in the manufacture: Pernod has a unique character of distilled aniseed of which the base is a 'spirit' prepared from fifteen regional plants, whose dosage constitutes the secret of manufacture. On the other hand, Pastis is produced by maceration, including aniseed essence and liquorice powder (from a plant from the Urals, the Caucasus or Turkey). Another important difference is found in the flavour and colour of each product, Pernod with the dominating aniseed flavour produces an opalescent green water mixture, whereas Pastis, with its aniseed and liquorice flavour, gives an opalescent white water mixture.

A French doctor, Dr Ordinaire, thought it a good idea to put a considerable distance between himself and the French Revolution, and therefore went to Switzerland, where he opened his practice at Couvert. He was something of a character and used to roam the mountains on a horse to collect aromatic plants, from which he made a secret elixir for stomach illnesses. On his death he bequeathed the secret to his housekeeper who, with two friends, started growing the plants in her garden.

Soon the elixir became popular in the region, and no one pretended that it was only invalids who bought it; the impressive manufacture of sixteen bottles a day was reached! A certain Major Dubied bought the recipe to offer as dowry for his daughter, who was going to marry Mr Henri-Louis Pernod. The die was cast, and Henri-Louis Pernod passed into posterity.

Anisette

Most liqueur compounders produce aniseed liqueurs, which are sweetened aniseed on a pure spirit base. The most famous is produced by Marie Brizard, of Bordeaux. Marie Brizard, who was born in 1714, inherited a secret formula for the production of anisette from a West Indian she successfully nursed back to health from the ravages of an epidemic. Halfway through the eighteenth century she and her nephew, Jean-Baptiste Roger, manufactured this and other liqueurs commercially. Their company is now acknowledged as one of the founders of the modern French liqueur industry. The distillery is still family-owned, and their products are world-renowed.

Anis del Mono

Spanish aniseed liqueur produced in Barcelona. It is water-white and is made in dry and sweet varieties.

Anisetta Stellata

Italian aniseed liqueur produced by the Aurum distillery in Pescara.

Elixir de China

Sweet, water-white Italian aniseed liqueur.

Escarchado

Portuguese aniseed liqueur containing sugar crystals.

La Tintaine

A French herb liqueur with a predominating aniseed flavour. It is presented in a bottle with a fennel stem, which gives a tree effect.

Ginepy

A local absinthe from the Val d'Aosta, produced in white and green.

Mastic, Masticha

Sweet white Greek and Cypriot liquorice-flavoured liqueurs. They are made from aniseed and the sap from trees of the cashew family. One of the finest comes from the island of Chios.

Mastika

Dry Balkan anis liqueur made from the gum of the mastic bush.

Ojen

Spanish absinthe-type liqueur.

Ouzo

White Greek and Cyprus anisette liqueurs which are drier than the north European types. Ouzo is normally drunk on the rocks, when it turns milky with the water. Douzico is the Macedonian dialect form of *ouzo*.

The quality of Ouzo is very much dependent on the country of origin. Ouzo can be produced by cold flavouring spirit with aniseed (*Princpinella anisum*) or by distillation of pure aniseed-flavoured spirit.

Oxygenee

Aniseed-flavoured absinthe substitute made in France and the U.S.A.

Raki

Aniseed and liquorice-flavoured Turkish liqueur, drunk with ice and water. The name has become generic for eastern Mediterranean liqueurs of these ingredients.

Sambuco

Water-white Italian liqueur combining the freshness of witch elderbush with liquorice flavour.

Tres Castillos

A Puerto Rican anisette liqueur sweetened with sugar candy.

Kümmel

Caraway seeds are excellent aids to digestion, which we eat in cakes and bread and use to flavour liqueurs. The properties of caraway have been known for centuries and the plant was profusely cultivated in Holland in the Middle Ages. Even today, we can enjoy caraway-flavoured cheeses and rye bread, and in our cradles we probably enjoyed the weakly alcoholic caraway-flavoured liquid called gripe water.

The earliest recorded European caraway liqueur was made by Lucas Bols in his small Amsterdam distillery in 1575—Bolskümmel is still famous. Lucas Bols was a man of dedicated talent who brought original skills to his trade. He gathered from many regions natural ingredients through which he passed alcoholic vapours to produce new and subtle scents, and it is claimed that his was probably the oldest distillery in the world.

The movement of Kümmel distillation from west to east Europe is believed to be a result of the travels of Peter the Great of Russia, who visited Amsterdam in 1696. Being anxious to establish a Russian Navy, he decided to learn ship-building at first hand, and worked as a labourer, keeping his identity secret. During his eighteen-month stay, he visited the Bols distillery and thus it is believed that he brought Kümmel to Russia. Production did not, in fact, commence until the early part of the nineteenth century with manufacture at the Allasch distillery.

Mentzendorff Kümmel originated as a family recipe of the Baron von Blanckenhagen, made at his stately home at Allasch Manor in Livoura, some twenty-five miles from Riga. The fame of this liqueur led a Riga firm, Mentzendorff, to suggest to the Baron's family that they should produce this excellent drink, then known as Allasch Kümmel, for export. Allasch castle then became the distillery where the liqueur was made in 1823.

By the First World War, Mentzendorff Kümmel was world renowned. With the end of the Russian empire, the large estates in the newly formed Baltic states were confiscated and Allasch was among the sufferers. The Blanckenhagen family moved first to Schwerin in Mecklenburg and then to Amsterdam, but they always controlled the manufacture of their liqueur and, like all good liqueurists, guarded the secrets of its composition.

Famous Riga Kümmels were made by the Wolfschmidt family, who were represented in England from the middle of the nineteenth century by Maurice Meyer and later by his daughter, the late Mrs Mary Fisher, who took over his business on his death in 1918. From that time on she devoted herself to the building up of the firm, Maurice Meyer, of which she remained managing director until her retirement in 1961. She died two years later, aged eighty-three.

In her early years in business she found the position rather strange, for in those days such a career for a woman was most unusual. Her ability, industry and perspicacity soon achieved for her a niche which she occupied with distinction for the rest of her life. She had a remarkable palate and her opinion was frequently sought. After she had been in business for some time, she decided to specialize in liqueurs and acquired a great reputation as an expert in this branch of the trade. Before the Second World War she listed nearly two hundred liqueurs, most of them from Europe, and some from other parts of the world. Her knowledge was fully recognized by her friends in the trade, and she frequently lectured on liqueurs. She was the author of the first book on the subject of liqueurs and often contributed to magazines and newspapers, and also broadcast.

Wolfschmidt made several types of Kümmel, which were all available in the United Kingdom until the Second World War:

Allasch type—typical Kümmel liqueur, sold at 72° proof.

Jagd Kümmel—hunting Kümmel sold in stone jars with highly colourful labels depicting hunting scenes; sold at 87° proof.

Dry unsweetened Kümmel, sold at 86° proof.

Crystallized Kümmel OO, sold at 97° proof.

Crème de Cumin, the finest of all Kümmel, was sold 103° proof in thin crystal bottles with a large pointed punt on which were formed sugar crystals giving the appearance of a snow covered mountain. Cumin is a dwarf plant of Egyptian origin related to the caraway family and cultivated throughout southern Europe. Another famous pre-war Kümmel was the Eckau OO of Count Pahlen.

The finest Kümmels of today are made in Holland, including the Wolfschmidt brand. This is a consequence of the disappearance of Latvia. Other recognized brands are Mentzendorff, Fockink and Bols, but of course, most distillers produce a Kümmel.

Gilka Kümmel

Drier than Allasch and the best known of the type classified as Berliner Kümmel, now produced in Hamburg. Gilka quality has been acknowledged for over 130 years.

C.L.O.C. (Cumin Liquidum Optimum Castelli)

A fine Danish caraway liqueur, literally 'the best caraway in the castle'. It is water-white and, at 31 per cent, weaker than Dutch Kümmel.

Danzig Goldwasser

This has been produced in Danzig by the firm of Der Lachs since 1598 and today's bottle is still embossed with the picture of a salmon (*der Lachs*).

The original sweet liqueur was water-white, flavoured with aniseed and caraway, the gold flakes only being added when it became known that gold was valuable in the treatment of certain diseases. In India, in the palaces of great princes, gold dust used to be sprinkled on sweet courses at important functions, to honour the guest and to aid digestion, and it is not surprising that considerable quantities of Der Lachs were sold to India before the war.

Since wartime destruction of the Der Lachs establishment in Danzig, the liqueur is now produced in West Berlin to the original Danzig formula.

Danzig Silberwasser

Identical to Danzig Goldwasser, with silver leaves instead of gold flakes. Although the flavour is identical, this version appears far less palatable with silver than with gold.

Liqueur d'Or

Most French and Dutch manufacturers now produce Goldwater, Garnier in France being the first in 1890.

24
Mint Liqueurs

The digestive properties of the various types of mint have long been known, and the most used variety in liqueurs, *Labiatae*, belongs to the same sweet herb family as garden mint.

Every liqueur producer manufactures Crème de Menthe, a mint- or peppermint-flavoured spirit sweetened and sold white or coloured green. Mitcham, in Surrey, was supposed to grow the finest mint and continental distillers imported it from there. The best-known green variety is 'Freezomint', made by Cusenier, who have been making liqueurs for over a hundred years, starting from the family home in the Jura mountains. They eventually moved to Paris. Eighty years ago they built a second distillery in Marseilles and today their products are world-renowned.

A second popular brand is Pippermint of Get Frères, in its own uniquely shaped bottle, available in green and white.

Royal Mint-Chocolate

See p. 152.

Mentuccia

'Little piece of mint' is also known as Centerbe, because it is said to be compounded from a hundred herbs gathered at the foot of the Abruzzi mountains, which produce a potent fine-flavoured digestive. It is sometimes known after its inventor, Fra. San Silvestro.

Vandermint

A Dutch minted chocolate liqueur marketed in painted Delft-style bottles.

25

Bean and Kernel Liqueurs

Crème de Cacao, or chocolate liqueur, is produced by all manufacturers making the full range of liqueurs, either by maceration or percolation of cacao beans followed by distillation and sweetening. It used to be very popular in the Far East, where it was drunk through a thick layer of cream floating on its surface. It is still extremely popular in the Marseilles area, and for restaurateurs it is most useful for serving with desserts and ice-cream sweets.

Crème de Cacao is available colourless or brown, the latter often including a little vanilla and stating on the label 'Crème de Cacao a la vanille'.

Several Crèmes de Cacao have the additional title Chouao. In the late nineteenth century, the finest cacao beans were grown in a valley near Caracas, in the Chouao valley, which was some dozen miles long and surrounded by forest-covered mountains. The colony was founded by monks; the wood from the forest was used to make fine furniture. Now Chouao is a suburb of Caracas, and although the term Chouao is still used on labels, this is now the generic term for Venezuelan cacao beans, as no more beans come from the original Chouao valley.

Chocolat Suisse

A well-known Swiss chocolate liqueur with floating chocolate pieces, by Marmot.

Cacao mit Nuss

A white German liqueur produced from chocolate with hazel-nut flavour. Also produced in Switzerland (with almonds) and in France (Royal Nut-Chocolate Liqueur).

Royal Mint-Chocolate

This is a new liqueur which reproduces the exquisite and delicate flavour of the after-dinner mint.

H. Warner Allen wrote in *Liqueurs and the Wine Lover*: 'To my amazement and delight when I tried it with my coffee my tongue and palate registered nothing but approval. The coarseness of chocolate had been extracted and the delicate flavour of the cacao berry, which I had not tasted for so many years that I had forgotten it, had been retained. This pleasant, smooth liqueur set me wondering how two tastes to which I thought I was allergic could have been so miraculously adapted to please my palate and came to the conclusion that it was a case of art returning to nature.'

Royal Mint-Chocolate liqueur took me about two years to develop. During the course of compounding, I found that making liqueurs is an art rather than a science, and that the invention of a new liqueur could best be paralleled with a composer working on an orchestral composition. The composer knows the sound he is hearing in his mind, and he is then able to pull it apart, giving each member of the orchestra a certain part to play. Similarly, with a liqueur, the final result is visualized; this is theoretically taken apart and then actually put together component by component to give the end-product. The compounding of a liqueur, of course, presents particular difficulties as the 'players' (special extracts, distillates, etc.) very often interact, giving very different results, and what is not generally realized is that the sequence of events is of extreme importance. As so often happens, it was pure chance that led to the final result in this case; a dozen independent unsuccessful trials had been mixed at the end of an evening and set aside for kitchen use in preparation of sweets and sorbets. When after a week, by chance, the mixture was tasted, the research was at an end! The answer had been found.

Extensive calculations were then necessary to break down the numerous components into exact quantities, and shortly after, with minor adjustments, 'Royal Mint-Chocolate' liqueur was born. It is now produced and bottled in France. Since 1966 the series has been increased into a 'Royal family' of liqueurs: Orange-Chocolate, Ginger-Chocolate, Cherry-Chocolate, Banana-Chocolate, Raspberry-Chocolate, and the Royal Jubilee liqueur,

Bean and Kernel Liqueurs

Lemon-Chocolate, all of which are discussed in the relevant sections of this book. Royal Apricot Chocolate and Royal French Coffee-Chocolate liqueurs were introduced in 1979, Royal Nut-Chocolate and Royal Fruit and Nut-Chocolate liqueurs in 1980 and Royal Coconut Chocolait in 1981.

COFFEE LIQUEURS

Crème de Café, Crème de Mokka are made in all liqueur-producing countries. The liqueurs are usually sweetened spirit extracts of coffee, coloured brown. Several have become extremely well known.

Tia Maria

A Jamaican rum liqueur based on Blue Mountain coffee extracts and local spices. The present liqueur was developed by Dr Kenneth Evans from an age-old recipe whose composition is a closely guarded secret.

Kahlúa

Mexican coffee liqueur which, for European markets, is made under licence by Heering in Denmark. The liqueur is quite different in style from Tia Maria and is very popular in the U.S.A.

Royal French Coffee-Chocolate Liqueur

A highly original double flavoured liqueur made in France with rich milk.

Gallweys Irish Coffee Liqueur

A smooth, dark brown liqueur with a rich coffee flavour. It is whiskey-based and partly uses old honey and herb recipes to blend with fragrant coffee.

Café Bénédictine

A recently introduced blend of coffee and Bénédictine.

Old Jamaica Blue Mountain Coffee Liqueur

Dr Sangster's strongly flavoured rum and coffee liqueur.

Kukul

A Mexican brand name for coffee and chocolate liqueurs.

Crème de Café—'Coffee Sport'

A light, fresh American coffee liqueur made by Jacquin and presented in a heat-resistant coffee pot which can be re-used for real coffee.

Coffee House Liqueur

A rich liqueur with the robust flavour of Virgin Islands spirit blended with local coffee extracts.

Bahia

Brazilian coffee blended with local grain spirit with a slightly bitter-sweet tang. Sold in a specially shaped bottle.

Coloma

A new Colombian coffee liqueur.

Mokka Mit Sahne

German coffee liqueur with cream (which must have a 10 per cent fat content).

Kirsch Mit Mokka

Coffee and cherry flavoured liqueur made from coffee extracts, cherry juice, plus Kirsch (and Framboise).

Mount Kenya Liqueur

A fine coffee liqueur made from Kenyan coffee, locally produced alcohol and a 'secret formula'.

Old Vienna Coffee Brandy

A blend of carefully selected coffee extracts and fine matured Cognac produced by Julius Meini in Vienna.

Also well known are Expresso (Italy), Aloha (Scotland) and Pasha (Turkey). There are several mokka and coffee liqueurs from Austria and Germany.

Noyau

A strong sweet liqueur, almond in flavour, which is made from extracts of peach and apricot kernels. There are several producers who offer the liqueur water-white or pink. The finest is the French of Vve Champion, which has been shipped to Maurice Meyer Ltd in London for over 100 years. The company still has Bills of Lading showing shipments of several products from Vve Champion dated 1869 and 1872.

It is recorded that the original M. Champion came from Martinique and established a distillery in Bordeaux. After his death, over 130 years ago, his widow made over the business to two of her workers, Droz and Jourde, and eventually Alexander Droz became the sole proprietor. His grandson continued to manufacture Vve Champion Noyau until his recent death. Happily the formula survives.

Kola Liqueurs

Made from kolanuts, citrus peel flavours, tonka beans and vanilla. Spices may also be added.

Crème de Vanille

A smooth, rich liqueur made from vanilla beans.

Cocoribe

A liqueur made from wild island coconut and Virgin Island Rum.

Malibu

A very successful recent liqueur made from coconut and light Jamaica Rum.

Coconut Whisqueur

A Scotch whisky-based coconut liqueur produced for manufacture of liqueur chocolates.

Afrikoko

Coconut and chocolate liqueur made in Sierra Leone and other African States.

Royal Coconut 'Chocolait'

Coconut and chocolate smoothly blended with rich French milk.

26

Flower, Blossom and Leaf Liqueurs

Japanese Green Tea Liqueur

A uniquely oriental liqueur. It is made from two fine teas—
Matcha, powdered tea, and Gyokuro, rolled tea—which have
been grown in Japan for centuries. The combination with grape
brandy gives a delightful liqueur, with a subtle perfume of fine
tea. Presentation is usually in ceramic bottles. Another tea liqueur
is Ocha.

Not many European producers market a Crème de Thé any
longer, although I recall tasting 'Tea Breeze' by Marie Brizard,
a medium dry, brown liqueur with a taste of spiced tea.

Tiffin

A German liqueur made from Darjeeling tea.

Cherry Blossom Liqueur

Unique to the Japanese house of Suntory, who are also large
producers of malt whiskey. The delicate pink liqueur is said to
capture the very essence of fragrant and precious cherry blossoms
and to mirror their mysterious bouquet.

Crème de Roses

Fine delicate French rose liqueur produced from the essential
oils extracted from rose petals. Small quantities of vanilla and
citrus oils are normally added. Gul is a Turkish brand.

Crème de Violettes

A sweet liqueur made from the petals of violets. Crème Yvette,
the best known, is the property of Jacquin, in Philadelphia. It was

named in honour of the famous French actress, Yvette Gilbert, at the turn of the century.

Benoit manufacture an Armagnac-based purple product.

Maple Liqueur

A unique Canadian liqueur made from the syrup of the maple tree, by Rieder in Ontario. The maple trees are tapped so that the sap slowly drips into collecting vessels. Brandy is added and the liqueur allowed to 'marry' before sale.

27
Miscellaneous Liqueurs

Advocaat

A thick, creamy liqueur made from the yolks of newlaid eggs and pure spirit. It is the lowest strength 'liqueur' available (approx. 17 per cent). Because of its low strength, in the past it had its own Customs descriptive category. Many recipes include small quantities of kirsch, vanilla and citrus peel extracts to enhance the flavour.

At the time of writing, an unresolved legal dispute exists between Dutch and English manufacturers as to whether 'Advocaat' should be made from spirit and eggs or from fortified wine and eggs.

Best known are the Dutch advocaats of Bols, Oud, Warnink, de Kuyper 'Black Hen' and the Channel Isles Guernsey Cream. Seagers Egg Nog is based on Australian fortified wine. Advocaat is particularly popular in mixed drinks with sparkling lemonade (Snowball).

I have enjoyed an excellent German lemon-flavoured advocaat, but was not impressed with a mokka-flavoured advocaat, although this and chocolate-flavoured advocaat appear to be popular in Germany. Rum-flavoured advocaats are popular on the Continent.

Atholl Brose

Not, strictly speaking, a liqueur but a Scottish drink whose origins go back two centuries. It is composed of Highland malt whisky, uncooked oatmeal made into a brose, honey, cream and secret ingredients to give the special flavour.

Baerenfang

German honey liqueur based on neutral spirit with extra flavouring from lime flowers and mullein flowers. A Polish honey liqueur is called Krupnick; a lime liqueur Crema de Lima is made in Spain.

Crème de Noisettes

The most famous nut liqueur is distilled in Orleans by Meyer. Distilled from hazel nuts specially selected for the delicacy of their flavour, the liqueur is sweetened and bottled with a floating hazel nut.

Crème de Noix

Walnut trees are widely grown in south-western France. The liqueurs from the local produce are a Pergourdine speciality—delicate, but with a rough charm.

Nocino

An Italian speciality from Sassuolo and Luzzara in Emilia, produced by the infusion of tender nut husks in pure spirit. Frequently used to flavour ice-cream.

Royal Nut-Chocolate, Royal Fruit and Nut-Chocolate Liqueurs

French reproductions of very popular flavours in British confectionery.

Frangelico

An Italian wild hazelnut berry and herb liqueur.

Crème d'Amandes

Almond liqueurs, usually sweet.

Donjon aux Amandes

Very nutty, spirity French almond liqueur.

Marnique

An Australian quince-based liqueur.

Okhotnichya 'Hunter's Brandy'

High-strength (77° proof) Russian brandy made by infusion of numerous materials, including citrus peel, ginger, galingale, clove, peppers, juniper, coffee and aniseed.

Reishu

Japanese melon liqueur.

Ponche

A very popular brown Spanish liqueur, with a pleasing reminiscence of fine old sherry. The firm de Soto present theirs in a silvered bottle decorated with a silken tassel.

Tryayos Devinerios

An old Lithuanian brandy famous for its medicinal properties.

Crème de Genième

This is made from distilled macerated juniper berries, matured and sweetened to give a lightly flavoured liqueur.

Alchermes

A traditional red Italian speciality, produced by the Carthusian monks of St Maria Novella. Produced from pure spirit, cinnamon, coriander, nutmeg, orris root and vanilla, it is scented with extracts of roses and jasmine.

Dairy Liqueurs

In the early 1970s two American producers, Heublein ('Hereford Cows') and Old Boston ('Aberdeen Cows'), marketed a range of mixed drinks that sold very well in their own country. It was, however, Baileys that created a world-wide interest in pure dairy cream liqueurs, a marketing idea that has swept the liqueur world. A delicately flavoured cream and Irish whiskey liqueur, offered at low strength, it has a magic appeal and may well become the world's largest selling liqueur. Many other Irish Creams are being marketed—Carolans, Tara, O'Darby, Waterford, Ryans—with different tastes appealing to different audiences. Italian (Venetian Cream), German (Chantré), Scottish (Heather Cream) and Dutch and Australian cream liqueurs are also produced.

For my own 'Royal' series, I have preferred to use rich French milk and to produce specifically flavoured liqueurs—Coffee-

Chocolate, Coconut-Chocolate—which are rich, but less so than the cream liqueurs. The latest addition is Alexanders, a new flavour including Scotch Whisky.

The popularity of dairy liqueurs has created phenomenal interest in all liqueurs, and manufacturers are delighted with this added stimulus to the general promotion of all liqueurs.

Fig Liqueurs

Several North African fig products are made and offered either as an *eau-de-vie* (Boukha Bokobsa) or sweetened as a liqueur such as Thitarine, which, apart from a distinctive fig flavour, also has a herb and liquorice taste.

Riemerschmid, a German manufacturer, offers his produce in a fig-shaped bottle.

Tamara

An Israeli date liqueur, packaged in a unique date-shaped bottle.

Gebürgs Polingen

A German mushroom liqueur.

Midori

A very successful Japanese musk melon liqueur.

Viennese Pear

A fine-flavoured Austrian liqueur.

PART III

28
Cocktails

Cocktails are short drinks made by mixing spirit with fruit juice or other flavours, and adding ice. They are shaken or stirred, then poured into decorated glasses and garnished with cocktail cherries or pieces of fruit to make them more attractive.

Mixed drinks originally developed in bars and the Bartenders' Guilds in many countries have created their own folklore in producing new concoctions and creating customer interest in new tastes and flavours. A cocktail, having several ingredients, must be produced so that the result is a palatable, very pleasant and attractive drink but it is important that the ingredients should totally harmonize so that none should overshadow the others.

Cocktails have always been more popular in the United States than anywhere else in the world, although many modern liqueur producers are now recommending that their products be used either in cocktails or new-style long drinks. The cocktail age began after the First World War, and during the inter-war period many thousands of recipes were produced; many with delightful names, many to be only shaken by their inventors; but only a few have stayed in the international repertoire and it is essential for every bartender to be able to prepare these without reference to a recipe book. It is, of course, very likely that the impetus for cocktail-shaking in America was created by Prohibition, a period during which home-made spirits were in constant production, many of which had an unpleasant bouquet and taste that could be well hidden in a mixed drink or cocktail.

There are many legends regarding the origin of the term cock-tail. Perhaps the most popular one relates to Betsy's Tavern, which was a meeting place for French and American officers of

Washington's army in 1779. There, the Irish barmaid—Betsy Flanagan—decorated her special drinks with the feathers from a cock's tail and it is said that one of the Frenchmen calling for a toast exclaimed '*vive le cocktail*', after which all of Betsy's concoctions were called cocktails. Another is that a chemist in New Orleans entertained his friends with mixed drinks which he served in double-ended egg cups, *coquetiers*, which the Americans turned into 'cockters' and, thereafter, cocktail. There is also the legend, of American origin, of a barkeeper who used a small natural root known as cola de tallo, from its shape, which was translated as cock's tail.

Whatever the origin of the word, it is known that mixed drinks have been popular for over 150 years; in 1806 an American journal, *Balance*, described a mixed drink, which we should now call a cocktail, as 'a stimulating liquor' composed of spirits of any sort, sugar, water and bitters. An American bartender, Jerry Thomas, published his mixed drink guide just over a hundred years ago, and in 1882 Harry Johnson published his illustrated bartenders' manual.

In the 1930s the Savoy Cocktail book was first published, as was the *Bartender*, the journal of the United Kingdom Bartenders' Guild, which has taken on the gigantic task of collating and indexing the many recipes which were produced and still are being produced; the Guild also monitors many international competitions to ensure that the recipes submitted are new and not re-named older mixtures.

The most famous of all cocktails is undoubtedly the Martini, which started life as the Martinez Cocktail based on Professor Jerry Thomas's original recipe which read: 'one dash of bitters, two dashes Maraschino liqueur, one pony Old Tom Gin, one wine glass vermouth, two small lumps of ice, shake, strain, garnish, etc.' But in due course it became the Martini and a mixture of equal parts of dry gin and dry vermouth; gradually, over the years, the mixture has contained less and less vermouth so that today's really dry Martinis are almost all gin with just the wave of a vermouth bottle cork over the glass!

The various types of cocktails and mixed drinks can be classified into many types, the main ones being:

Cocktails

Collins	Highballs	Scaffes
Crustas	Juleps	Shrubs
Daisies	Pick-me-ups	Slings
Egg Nogs	Pousse Café	Smashes
Fixes	Puff	Sours
Fizzes	Punches	Swizzle
Flips	Rickeys	Toddies
Floats	Sangarees	Zooms
Frappés		

There is no doubt that these mixed drinks provide a new excitement in drinking; an endless combination of flavours are being produced that encourage adventure in drinking. The new interest in liqueurs, mixed drinks and cocktails has helped to overcome the traditional seasonality of these fine products, and they are heavily promoted by manufacturers everywhere.

29
Cooking with Liqueurs
by Elaine Hallgarten

Cooking with wines has long been accepted practice, but mention using liqueurs or spirits in the kitchen and an air of the somewhat wicked is introduced. The possible explanation for this attitude is economical. After all, a bottle of wine is, happily, still not considered outrageously extravagant, whereas spirits and liqueurs are very much in the luxury class, due to heavy taxation. A moment's reflection can put the whole thing into perspective however. Where you might need a bottle of château something or other to make a *Coq au Vin*, you will need only a tablespoon or so of brandy in the same dish. And to make a stunning dessert may require a mere splash or two of liqueur, thus giving an exotic touch out of all proportion to the expense involved.

Many of the producers of liqueurs publish booklets of recipes and the serious student of these matters would be well advised to acquire a selection. These excellent publications suggest using liqueurs in adventurous ways, but it would be a brave cook who would hazard a heavy, sweet liqueur, however judiciously added, with cheesy chicken or a salmon quiche, as suggested by one manufacturer. More conservatively, you may be more enthusiastic about employing a little spirit in a *Poulet Val d'Auge*, which calls for Calvados, or a shot of brandy to liven up a casserole of beef. Terrines and pâtés often include spirits, to improve both the flavour and the keeping properties.

Liqueurs are generally sweet, and therefore their use in cooking is most likely to be in the dessert rather than the main course. Some liqueurs go naturally with particular food, matching their subtle flavours to one special ingredient. An obvious partnership is Grand Marnier (or any of the many other orange-flavoured liqueurs) with any orange dish. Calvados goes with apples; the bean or kernel type of liqueurs can enhance chocolate, coffee or cream desserts.

Fruit-based liqueurs are perhaps the most versatile in cooking, although many recipes using liqueurs are quite suitable for almost any type of liqueur. There's nothing more aggravating than planning to make a particular recipe, only to discover that you have only two drops of the specified liqueur. Certainly soufflés, although frequently made with Grand Marnier, are equally delicious, and equally impressive, made with almost any other liqueur you have to hand. You therefore only need to know the basic recipe, adding the required amount of your chosen liqueur. Since soufflés are invariably treated with hushed reverence, and offered at vastly inflated prices in most restaurants, perhaps it is worth noting that they are surprisingly simple to make and economical into the bargain. The mystique of soufflés has long been exploded—it must have been all those draughty kitchens and unregulated ovens which caused so many disasters. They are actually quite robust and can be prepared up to four hours before cooking, refrigerating them until they are popped into the oven. You can even open the oven door to see how they are getting along. The only essential is that your guests are ready to eat the masterpiece, which waits, like time, for no man.

A basic mousse recipe can also be adapted for many different liqueurs, adding a complementary ingredient if you like. For instance, a Royal Ginger-Chocolate mousse, with some finely chopped stem ginger, is one possibility, while a Crème de Cassis mousse with some fresh blackcurrants is a variation on the same theme.

Although the orange liqueurs have a particular affinity with oranges, it is sometimes more interesting to make less obvious partnerships. Caramel oranges, which are always a popular sweet, are delicious with the addition of a Scotch liqueur, rather than Cointreau or Curaçao. Thinly sliced pineapple, which many people associate with Kirsch, is also excellent with whisky liqueur. This same liqueur is good with creamy syllabubs or mousses, as are other herb-based liqueurs. A small quantity of, say, Bénédictine, added to the cream filling of an ordinary sponge cake, can make it into an extraordinary dessert.

Almost any liqueur is suitable to add to a fruit salad. A lively idea is to marinade individual fruits in a matching liqueur or spirit—apples in Calvados, plums in slivovitz, apricots in brandy, cherries in Maraschino or Kirsch, then mix them together. The resulting salad will prove to be an extremely potent fruit cocktail. Prunes, which many people find revive childhood memories of nursery food, take on quite a different flavour when steeped in Armagnac. Other fruits can be bought bottled in this spirit and make delicious additions to a winter fruit salad. A very simple dessert, using the luscious produce of the Normandy countryside, is a thick purée of apples laced with a dash of Calvados and served with the heaviest cream you can find. A truly exquisite finale to a meal.

For those with a dramatic turn of mind, and the right equipment to hand, flambéeing fresh fruit is bound to be a success. All you need is a table heater, a small frying-pan, some spirit or liqueur and prepared fruit. Pineapple with Kirsch, bananas with rum, peaches with brandy and oranges with any of the kindred spirits would all make exciting eating. While you have the equipment out, you could use it to ignite a few *crêpes*, in a sauce of lemon juice, orange juice and brandy. If you are the shy, retiring type, you can be as gastronomically successful discreetly warming the *crêpes* through in a sauce in the kitchen. A chocolate sauce spiked with a suitably chocolate-flavoured liqueur would make a delightful change, both for *crêpes* and over pears. Poire Hélène, which should be the most gorgeous of desserts, is so often spoiled by being served swathed in a stodgy, cold, blancmange-type sauce.

As a topping for ice-creams, liqueurs are the ideal quick answer. The bean or kernel type of liqueurs are particularly suitable and, for fruit ices, the fruit-based liqueurs make excellent partners. A superb way to take in your daily requirement of milk and eggs is to make an egg nog, laced with brandy or a mixture of Bourbon and brandy. Another liquid refreshment which readily accepts a 'dosage' of liqueur or spirits is the milk shake.

Frozen desserts which include liqueurs are very popular, surprisingly even in winter. For the host or hostess there is a comforting feeling in having a few delicious goodies tucked into the freezer ready for unexpected guests. The great advantage of most frozen desserts is that they are eaten straight from the freezer—instant pudding was never like this. A point to remember when serving frozen desserts which include liqueurs—alcohol lowers the freezing point of the mixture and therefore the desserts melt very quickly once they have been removed from the freezer. It is essential to serve them quickly and return any that is left over to the freezer before it disintegrates.

Spirits and liqueurs should perhaps be marketed as the ultimate in convenience drinks—they need little or nothing with them, and provide a sure way to liven up any dish to which they are added. If you are short of time but need to provide a dessert out of the ordinary, add a dash of liqueur—to a custard sauce (*crème pâtissière*, preferably, but even one made with custard powder would be vastly improved); over ice-cream or into a hot sauce accompanying it; whisked into whipped cream—or try some of the following recipes.

Chicken Liver Pâté for 6 to 8

450 g (1 lb) chicken livers	2 tablespoons whisky or
1 medium onion	brandy
·1 bay leaf	1 teaspoon thyme
175 g (6 oz) butter	parsley
2 tablespoons sherry	2 cloves garlic
	salt and pepper

Sauté the chicken livers with the finely chopped onion and bay leaf in half of the butter. Purée the cooked livers in a blender with the remaining ingredients, except the butter. Melt the butter and add to the liver mixture. Blend again and put into a pot. Refrigerate overnight.

This pâté freezes very well. Wrap well. Defrost overnight in refrigerator.

Veal with Calvados for 6

700 g (1½ lb) veal escalope	300 ml (½ pint) single cream
(or smaller pieces)	4 tablespoons Calvados
2 cooking apples	salt and pepper
butter	

Season the veal well and brown in hot butter. Add the peeled and thinly sliced apples. Cook until the veal is tender and the apples softened. Warm the Calvados and pour over the meat. Warm the cream and add to the meat.

Serve immediately.

Frozen Grand Marnier Soufflé for 10

2 egg yolks
350 g (¾ lb) caster sugar
3 tablespoons water

600 ml (1 pint) whipping cream
4 tablespoons Grand Marnier

Beat the egg yolks until they are light and creamy. Put the sugar and water into a pan on a gentle heat. Stir until the sugar is dissolved and continue cooking until a thread is formed when the syrup drops from a fork.

Remove from the heat and slowly add the syrup to the beaten yolks. Beat for a further 5 minutes.

Whip the cream and fold into the egg mixture. Add the Grand Marnier. Turn the mixture into a soufflé dish. Cover with foil and freeze for at least 12 hours.

Serve from the freezer, decorated with whipped cream and crystallized violets.

Iced Royal Orange-Chocolate Soufflé for 4

4 egg yolks
3 egg whites
50 g (2 oz) granulated sugar
50 g (2 oz) caster sugar

2 lemons
pinch of salt
1½ tablespoons Royal Orange-Chocolate Liqueur

Place the yolks, lemon juice and some grated rind and the granulated sugar in a heavy saucepan and mix together well with a whisk. Place the saucepan on to a low heat and stir the mixture well until it becomes quite thick and glutinous. Take care not to let it overheat as this will cook the yolks.

Remove the pan from the heat and plunge it into a basin of cold water.

Beat the egg whites with the salt until they are very stiff, as for meringues. Slowly fold in the caster sugar and mix it in thoroughly. Scoop a spoonful of beaten whites into the yolk mixture and very gently fold it in. Continue to do this with the rest of the beaten whites until both mixtures are incorporated. Add the liqueur and mix through carefully. Spoon into four individual pots or one serving dish. Cover with foil and place in the freezer for a minimum of 6 hours.

Before serving, decorate with candied fruits or a thin slice of orange.

Frozen Marshallow Cake for 6

75 g (3 oz) digestive biscuits	75 g (3 oz) white marsh-
1 tablespoon cocoa	mallows
50 g (2 oz) butter	4 tablespoons Royal Mint-
125 ml (4 fl oz) milk	Chocolate Liqueur
150 ml (5 fl oz) double cream	green food colouring

Melt the butter and stir in the finely crumbled biscuits and cocoa. Mix well. Press into a foil-lined cake tin (preferably spring form).

Warm the milk with the marshmallows, stirring until they are dissolved.

Whip the cream until stiff. Fold it into the milk and marsh-mallow mixture. Add the liqueur and a few drops of green food colouring to make a soft shade of green.

Pour into the prepared case. Cover with foil and freeze for a minimum of 6 hours.

Serve direct from the freezer—do not defrost.

Liqueur Soufflé for 6

50 g (2 oz) butter	6 eggs
50 g (2 oz) flour	5 tablespoons liqueur
450 ml (¾ pint) milk	2 tablespoons sugar

Melt the butter and stir in the flour. Add the milk gradually, stirring all the time until the sauce is smooth and thick. Add the sugar and stir through. Remove from the heat.

Separate the eggs and stir the yolks into the sauce quickly. Add the liqueur. Beat the whites until very stiff and fold into the sauce.

Lightly butter a soufflé dish and sprinkle a little caster sugar around the dish. Turn the soufflé mixture into the dish.

At this stage you can refrigerate the soufflé for up to 4 hours before cooking it. If you do so, cook in a pre-heated oven set at 325° F. (gas Mark 3) for 50 minutes. If you are cooking the soufflé immediately after preparation, 40 minutes in the oven should be sufficient.

After the stated cooking time, carefully open the oven door and have a look at the soufflé. Test it as you do a cake and if the knife comes out almost clean, it's done. Otherwise give it a few minutes more. Before serving, dust the top with a little icing sugar.

Liqueur Mousse for 6

4 eggs	3 tablespoons boiling water
4 tablespoons caster sugar	4 tablespoons liqueur
1 tablespoon gelatine	

Separate the whites and yolks. Beat the yolks with the sugar until light and creamy. Dissolve the gelatine in the boiling water. Beat whites until stiff. Add the liqueur (and any complementary ingredients) to the yolk mixture and quickly add gelatine mixture, straining if necessary. Fold this mixture gently into the whites and pour into individual pots, or one large bowl. Refrigerate until required.

Decorate according to flavouring.

This mousse freezes well. Allow about 1 hour to defrost.

Variations: Grand Marnier, with some grated orange rind; Glen Mist; Coffee liqueur, with 100 g (4 oz) melted chocolate; Royal Ginger-Chocolate with chopped stem ginger; Crème de Cassis with blackcurrants.

Advocaat with Ginger for 4

5 tablespoons Advocaat	1 tablespoon chopped stem
200 ml (7 fl oz) double cream	ginger (or more to taste)

Softly whip the cream and add to the Advocaat. Stir in the ginger and mix through gently.

Refrigerate until required.

APPENDIXES

LIQUEUROGRAPH CHART
Liqueurs, Eaux-de-Vie and Spirits

◄── Approximate range per 30 ml ──

HERBS	**BRITISH**	Glen [l]
	EUROPEAN	Cuaranta-y-tres [31] Mille Fiori Parfait Amour (30) Ponche Soto [32] Dutch, French [43] Trappistine [40]
	SEED	[25] Anisette Greek Ouzo [37] [38] Ar M
	MINT	Dutch (30) Crème de Menthe (30) French Royal Mint-Chocolate
FRUIT	**CITRUS**	Van der Hum [31] Orange (40) Curaçao [30] Quartet [30] Royal Orange-Chocol Royal Lemon-Chocolat Paradiso [28·5]
	APRICOT PEACH	[24] Trotosky Apricot French Apricot Brandy (30) Royal Apricot-Chocolate [28·5] Brandy (30) Dutch Apricot Brandy
	CHERRY	Grant's Cherry Whisky, [25] [28·5] Scottish Royal [30] Brandy Cherry Whisky Cherry-Chocolate [24] Trotosky (24) Dutch Cherry Brandy [27] Maraschino French Cherry Brandy (24) [25] Cherry Heering [40] Wiśni
	ARCTIC FRUITS	[23] Suomuurain
	MISCELLANEOUS FRUITS	(17) Crème de Cassis Blackberry (30) (30) Crème de Fraises [27] Pedlar Sloe Gin Royal Raspberry-Chocolate [28·5] Blackcurrant Rum, [24] Royal Banana-Chocolate [30] Pineapple Rum Royal Coconut [21] Midori [23] Crème de Framboise (30) (17) Crème de Banane
BEAN & KERNEL	**COFFEE CHOCOLATE FRUIT KERNEL**	Kahlúa [26] [26] Tia Maria [34] Gallweys Malibu [28] Crème de Cacao (30) Royal Nut-Chocolate [28·5] Royal French Coffee-Chocolate [21] [30] Noyau Rose
SPIRITS	**FRUIT (EAUX-DE-VIE)**	Polish Slivovitz [40]
	GIN VODKA WHISKY WHISKEY BRANDY	[38/40] British Vodkas and Gins [46] Smirno Smirnov Wolfschmidt [38] [40] Geneva Polish Vodka [42] Scotch Whisky, Russian Vo American Whiskey, [40] Irish Whiskey Grape [38/40] Brandy
	RUM DARK WHITE	Jamaica, Demerara [40] [40] Appleton Estate Caror Imperial Diamond [40] [40] Daiquiri [40] Ron Bacardi

1982 5th Edition by Peter Hallgarten

Brontë 34

40 Drambuie

Glayva 40

Strega 40   42 Benedictine   43 Yellow Chartreuse   Green Chartreuse 55

36 Yellow Izarra   42 B & B   43 Vieille Cure

Iixir D'Anvers 38   Cordial Médoc 40   40 Galliano   49 Green Izarra

0 Pernod   40 Liqueur d'Or   40 Sambuca

9 Kummel

34 Sabra

Grand Marnier 39

40 Cointreau

39 Curaçao Triple Sec

40 Pimpeltjens, Mandarine Napoléon

Southern Comfort 43

French Peach Brandy

Kirsch Peureux 40

Mesimarja 23   28.5 Karpi

Cream Liqueurs
17 Baileys, Carolans, Waterford, Ryans, O'Darby, Royal Tara, Heather Cream, Chantré

Egg Liqueurs
Advocaat 17   Dutch, Guernsey and U.K.

○ Approx. strength of a liqueur type at various strengths by several distillers
70 = Alcohol % by volume

70 British Proof 80 U.S. proof 40% alcohol by volume

30 Amaretto di Saronno

Tequila   40 Kirsch d'Alsace   Framboise 45

40 Calvados 'Un Trou Normand'   Quetsch 45   Mirabelle 45   Poire William 43

5 Aquavit   57 Kosher White Spirit   56 Russian Krepkaya

57 Polish Spirit   Polish White Spirit 80

De Luxe   40 Armagnac   Fine Champagne Cognac,   Liqueur Cognac 40
Scotch   V.S.O.P. Cognac 40

57 Woods

Statistical Information about Scotch Whisky, Cognac and Armagnac

1 SCOTCH WHISKY

	PRODUCTION			SALES		
					U.K Con-	*Stocks*
	Malt	*Grain*	*Total*	*Exports*	*sumption*	*(31 March)*
1969	143,540	200,482	344,022	136,048,428	23,959,600	1,822,730
1970	148,600	222,078	370,678	160,914,668	27,338,300	1,975,570
1971	159,413	228,277	387,690	182,500,576	28,770,800	2,124,270
1972	176,245	258,776	435,021	178,411,396	32,652,900	2,249,610
1973	199,112	271,987	471,099	203,576,878	39,825,500	2,484,450
1974	214,669	261,726	476,395	227,336,065	45,075,200	2,637,560
1975	178,926	215,338	394,264	234,274,309	42,410,100	2,777,170
1976	167,411	194,854	362,265	238,302,745	48,438,300	2,814,280
1977	171,457	222,101	393,558	243,632,634	40,248,500	2,824,920
1978	209,279	250,020	459,299	274,072,934	48,812,000	2,860,210
1979	203,871	255,138	459,009	262,420,711	52,536,300	2,958,040
1980	177,913	237,957	415,870	249,916,996	50,158,800	3,048,400
	(× 1,000 litres pure alcohol)			(litres pure alcohol)		(1000 litres pure alcohol)

(Scotch Whisky Association)

Note: 1·5 proof gallons approx. 1 dozen bottles of whisky at 40/43 per cent.

2 COGNAC

	Production	Sales Export	Sales in France	Total Sales
1970/71	634·3	266·9	68·1	335·0
1971/72	421·9	268·1	72·6	340·7
1972/73	406·7	270·9	69·7	340·6
1973/74	740·3	230·4	60·0	290·4
1974/75	544·3	202·8	62·7	265·5
1975/76	720·1	241·2	81·6	322·8
1976/77	447·2	253·6	75·6	329·2
1977/78	354·5	247·6	76·4	324·0
1978/79	503·2	314·0	91·1	405·1
1979/80	655·4	339·9	84·5	424·5
1980/81	451·7	334·8	81·6	416·4

(× 1,000 hectolitres of pure alcohol)

3 ARMAGNAC

	Production	Sales Export	Sales in France	Total Sales
1971/72	37·30	—	13·88	—
1972/73	50·85	—	22·32	—
1973/74	116·96	—	22·83	—
1974/75	81·42	22·58	10·97	33·55
1975/76	58·28	19·98	20·38	40·36
1976/77	48·33	16·87	21·65	38·52
1977/78	12·52	19·14	24·50	43·64
1978/79	43·14	25·37	20·14	45·51
1979/80	87·15	22·42	21·63	44·05
1980/81	35·87	19·46	21·09	40·55

(× 1,000 in hectolitres of pure alcohol)
(Food from France)

Note: 1 hectolitre = 22 gallons approx.

1 hectolitre of pure alcohol produces approx. 330 bottles at normal consumer strength (40 per cent).

Index

Index